TANYA ANNE CROSBY

LION HEART

An Avon Romantic Treasure

AVON BOOKS
An Imprint of HarperCollinsPublishers

This is a work of fiction. Names, characters, places, and incidents are products of the author's imagination or are used fictitiously and are not to be construed as real. Any resemblance to actual events, locales, organizations, or persons, living or dead, is entirely coincidental.

AVON BOOKS
An Imprint of HarperCollins*Publishers*
10 East 53rd Street
New York, New York 10022-5299

Copyright © 2000 by Tanya Anne Crosby
Inside cover author photo by Clay Heatley
ISBN: 0-380-78575-7
www.avonromance.com

First Avon Books paperback printing: July 2000

Avon Trademark Reg. U.S. Pat. Off. and in Other Countries, Marca Registrada, Hecho en U.S.A.
HarperCollins® is a trademark of HarperCollins Publishers Inc.

Printed in the U.S.A.

WCD   10   9   8   7   6   5   4   3   2   1

Prologue

~~~~~~~~~~~~~~~~~~~~

Descended of the powerful sons of Mac-Alpin, the MacKinnon laird seemed invulnerable behind his veil of authority. But Broc knew better. The innocence of youth had been stripped from his child's mind; he no longer believed any man invincible.

His da was dead, his minny too, and he'd come to Chreagach Mhor a poor relation seeking refuge.

He stood tall, his father's enormous battle-scarred sword tucked into his belt, answering all of the MacKinnon's questions without shedding a tear, though he wished more than anything he could run away and find a quiet spot to patch his bleeding heart.

Though the MacKinnon had welcomed him with open arms, Broc knew he would never feel wholly part of this clan. His own kinsmen had been murdered, their lands razed, and he felt like a beggar now standing before the MacKinnon laird.

"The lad is welcome to remain," the Mac-Kinnon assured Broc's escort. "My wife's kin will always have a place among us. And I shall keep him safe as though he were my own."

The old woman cried out in gratitude. "Praise ye, good sir!"

Auld Alma had assisted nearly every birth in the MacEanraig clan for as long as Broc could recall. She, too, had been left homeless, without family, but Broc knew she wouldn't remain in the MacKinnon's care. Nay, Alma would return to sweep up the ashes. She would bury every poor soul she had helped bring into this world, and afterward she would remain to keep their graves.

"God will smile upon thee for this kindness!" she assured the MacKinnon.

Chreagach Mhor boasted the only stone keep in all of Scotia. Its laird seemed more a king than a simple chieftain, but his manner was far from imperious as he responded to her grief-stricken blessing. He smiled down at them from his seat upon the dais. His only son, Iain, sat on his lap, and the MacKinnon's fingers were laced in the boy's hair. Though Broc's throat grew thick at the sight of them, he didn't turn away.

He met Iain MacKinnon's gaze directly.

"And ye, too, may have a warm bed should ye choose to remain," the elder MacKinnon told Alma. "There is room enough. If not within the keep, surely elsewhere. We would welcome ye."

"Nay, sir." Alma shook her head adamantly. "But I thank ye anyway. I am auld, and my place is with my husband." Her eyes filled again with tears.

The elder MacKinnon nodded soberly and said nothing more. He knew, as Broc knew, that her husband was dead. They were all dead but for a few.

Clutching the hilt of his father's sword, he lifted his shoulder, catching a fat tear with his tunic. Och, but he wasn't a wee bairn anymore. He shouldn't weep. It was his duty to be strong. If only his heart would stop squeezing him so awfully. Another tear slipped past his guard, and he quickly swiped it away.

Dirty Sassenachs.

Anger dried his eyes.

He'd known them by their armor, bright silver shielding their bodies from their legs to the top of their heads. Like flawless mirrors, their helms had shone under the midmorning sun.

No Scotsman wore that costume of cowards.

No Scotsman worth bearing the name murdered wee bairns and expectant mothers for the sake of greed.

The pale-faced demons had come and gone as quickly as a sudden tempest. Broc had been too busy skipping stones into the loch to fight beside his family. He had shunned his duties that morn, had stolen away to play, and he would regret his childish decision for the rest of his years.

By the time their screams were heard, it was too late. From a distance, he'd first spied the smoke curling into the sky. And before his eyes, their homes had been reduced to ash. Never in his life had he felt such a rage. He'd run after them, trying to stop them, but the scoundrels had mounted their horses and ridden away like the cowards they were. His father had said they would not stop until all of Scotia was under King Henry of England's rules. As long as Broc lived he didn't think he would forget the scorched smell of his village as he'd come upon it. In his nightmares he would envision the slain bodies of his kinsmen lying limply among the mounds of ash that were once their homes.

In his heart he would dream of vengeance.

His little fist tightened upon the hilt of his father's heavy sword. Though he could barely carry it now, someday this very sword would exact vengeance for his mother's life and honor. There would never be room enough for other devotions. He would give his labors and his gratitude to the MacKinnon, but his heart would remain dark, lit only by the fires of revenge. Vengeance, like a glittering torch through a dark wood, would guide his way.

He would not be distracted by women or drink.

He would not be placated by holding a young bairn on his knee.

He didn't deserve to be surrounded by grandchildren in his old age.

He'd failed his mother.

He'd failed his kinsmen.

Aye, *they* had killed her, but he was as responsible as they were. He should have fought alongside his family.

Another tear rushed down his cheek.

He was big enough to defend his minny! He was big enough to defend his home! He should have died beside them. If it took the rest of his days to redeem himself, he would somehow find a way. He wasn't some weak, whey-faced Sassenach girly boy! He was big for his age, they said, and would grow up to be bigger and stronger than most.

And someday he would avenge his minny and his da.

Someday he would make the English pay for their murdering ways!

Iain MacKinnon slid down from his father's knee and came toward him. He was younger than Broc, though not by many years—perhaps five to Broc's seven, though Broc couldn't be certain. He came and stood before Broc, looking him square in the eyes. His expression was sober and somehow as dignified as his da's. He nodded and said, " 'Twill be alright, Broc Ceannfhionn."

Broc didn't think it true, but he didn't say so. He narrowed his eyes at the name Iain had bestowed upon him—Broc the Blond. No one had ever called him such a thing, but it didn't seem such a bad thing to be called. He nodded back, thanking Iain wordlessly for his words of comfort. Five was just too young to know anything at all. When the boy was seven at least, he would better understand.

"You can share my room," Iain offered. "I'll even show you where it is."

Broc peered up at Alma. He wanted to go with her, instead, to help put all the ghosts to rest.

She reached out to catch his chin, lifting his face. "Sweet Broc, ye'll do well here," she predicted.

Another tear slipped past his guard.

"Forget the anger, child," she advised him, "and remember the love. Make your sweet minny proud!" she commanded him. "Find ye a good woman to cherish and give her strong bairns. Let your father's blood live long in your veins and those of your children! You are the last of the MacEanraig clan, lad."

He swallowed hard, realizing he'd never see her again. His last tie to his kinsmen would be severed the instant she walked out the door.

But his da would want him to be a man.

He gazed at her tender countenance one last time, his eyes stinging sorely, but he didn't shed a single tear as he turned to follow Iain MacKinnon from the hall.

He would remember Alma's words always, but he never once looked back.

Chapter 1

A blackbird chased its mate across the sunlit sky. The pair fluttered together into a nearby tree, chirping merrily as lovers are wont to do.

Broc felt somehow empty at the sight of them. It was the second time during the span of the day that the feeling had come over him. He couldn't quite put his finger on what troubled him. He was restless.

It was a beautiful summer day with every tree a verdant green. The scent of something delightful but elusive hung in the air like an invisible mist, teasing his nostrils. Something like sweet pollen mayhap, though he couldn't name the flower of its birth.

He stopped to watch the birds upon a branch overhead. Furious little creatures, they struggled together as though battling. His brows drew together as he watched them pair off.

God's truth, it seemed everything and everybody was mating except him.

And he was the last of his clan.

It hadn't much bothered him before today. He hadn't allowed it. But after Gavin's sermon at Colin's and Seana's wedding, he found himself remembering an old woman's blessing.

Find ye a good woman to cherish and give her strong bairns. Let your father's blood live long in your veins and those of your children! You are the last of the MacEanraig clan, lad.

The echo of her voice had faded through the years. But her words had come back to haunt him.

They left him strangely bereft.

If someone had asked him only a few months before if Colin might ever wed, Broc would have laughed in their face and shaken his head with absolute conviction. But his best friend was now a married man, and Broc had never seen Colin so joyful. He was pleased for the both of them. And yet . . . in the aftermath of their nuptials, he found himself obsessing over an old woman's last words to him and craving something he couldn't name.

He turned away from the birds and continued on his journey home. In times past, Merry, his dog, would have been at his heels, and he might have had to drag her barking away from the damned tree.

He missed the sweet mutt.

He sighed and pushed her memory away, only to be besieged by another more poignant.

Always it hovered on the edge of his consciousness—the sound of his parents laughing together.

The two of them had been deeply devoted to each other, and his da had so obviously cherished his mother that as a child Broc had felt enriched by their love. But as happy as his childhood had been, despite the hardships, his memories were tainted with the hideousness of their death.

He could never think of them without remembering the other. . . .

He had no idea that he had stopped again, nor that he sat upon the ground, but he was left reeling by the images that accosted him. Even after all these years his kinsmen's faces haunted him. He plucked a woodland flower from the soil and crushed it in his fist, his gut burning with remembered rage.

God help him, it was better never to open one's heart at all, better never to be left so defenseless. The little boy he had been was long dead now. The man he had become was far stronger alone. His devotion was reserved for God and his clan, the clan that had embraced him as a child and made him one of its own. Aside from the clan, he didn't want to cleave to anyone.

A wife would be nought more than a burden— one he couldn't afford.

A dog's growl startled him from his reverie.

For an instant, he forgot Merry was dead and mistook the sound for that of his old companion. He turned, expecting to find her black eyes watching him, and instead saw a strange, overgrown hound instead. The animal's teeth were bared, but something about the eyes seemed docile and harmless, mayhap even afeared. Its coat was bedraggled, wet and dirty, mayhap from a trek through the bog. It was in desperate need of a bath, food and a warm place at someone's feet.

It was just so that he'd found Merry. He'd had to win her over, as well. The memory brought a wistful smile to his lips.

But then he thought about the way she'd died and how much it had hurt to lay her to rest, and that empty feeling returned.

It was too damned difficult to lose the things you loved, and it seemed to Broc that everything he loved most, he lost.

Some part of him wanted to rise up now and brush himself off, walk away from this beast, but he didn't. He sat there, making no move either to leave it or approach it.

The animal's bright eyes stared back at him.

Broc didn't avert his gaze. He tried to convey to the beast that no harm would come to it. He removed from the pouch at his waist a small sliver of smoked meat and offered it as a token of his friendship.

He spoke to it softly, and the animal laid its ears back, cocking its head curiously. Broc smiled and continued to gaze at it, willing it to come to him. Extending his hand, he began to coo to it, and soon it lowered its head and took a step forward.

It took yet another when Broc made no move to close the distance between them.

"That a girl," he crooned, though he had no idea of the sex of the beast. Gender didn't matter much with anything that traveled on four legs, he decided, as he waved the meat at the animal, cajoling it nearer.

It wasn't long before the dog was at his side, shaking its wet coat and spattering him in the face with stinky bog water. Broc chuckled and rubbed it vigorously, rewarding it for its bravery. He handed over the meat. The poor beast snatched it, devouring it in one gulp, then peered up at him as though expecting more.

Broc laughed, patting it. "There ye go," he said again, and stood, continuing to pet it. Its coat was soft, though it was damp and dirty. It was obviously hungry as well, but he had nothing else to feed it. Still, it looked up at him appreciatively, and his heart melted.

He was a fool for animals—they were loyal without fault and always grateful.

Who needed women when they were never appeased and rarely faithful?

Let Colin and Leith and Iain and the rest of the lads have their fill of them. He was better off alone. He wasn't about to saddle himself with some nagging, complaining bitch. Nay, a dog was all the companion he needed. If you tossed dogs a few scraps, they followed you till the day they died.

He should take this one home, he decided, as he stroked its head, feed it, mayhap bathe it, as well. He'd learned the merits of bathing his animals. His laird's wife had taught him how to rid the beasts of fleas, and since he didn't seem to be able to keep them off his bed, it served him well to heed her advice.

"Good lass," he said, and the animal lowered its head, enjoying his attentions. He wondered where the dog had come from and to whom it belonged. He didn't recall ever seeing it before today. Hungry it might be, but it didn't appear famished, so it couldn't have come very far. If it ran off after he cleaned it up a bit and fed it, he would certainly understand.

He started to walk away, hoping it would follow. The dog took a few steps, then stopped abruptly, and Broc stopped as well, determined to befriend it. And then all at once it began to bark as though it wanted him to stay.

Or mayhap follow.

"What is it, lass?" he asked and took a step toward it. The dog took a step back, and Broc scratched his head, trying to figure out what the moody beast was trying to tell him.

It must be a bitch, he decided, because she didn't seem to be able to make up her bloody mind whether she liked him or nay.

Chapter 2

E lizabet felt like ripping out her hair in frustration.

She tethered the mounts and sat, disheartened, upon the roots of an old oak to await these unruly men with whom her father had burdened her to travel with. She sighed and hugged her knees, wondering about her father's cousin.

Would Piers welcome them warmly?

Or would he eye them as her father's new wife had, like some viper trying to slither into her home?

God's truth, she was weary and just about as snappish as her mother's dog—which by the by was gone again! And the men were off doing God knew what! And on top of everything else, they were lost, and no one seemed the least inclined to stop and ask for directions.

They'd passed a small hut a furlong back, with a kindly-looking old woman standing before it. What harm could the old woman possibly have done to five burly soldiers? Well, four—her half-brother wasn't quite burly. Most likely, a simple, polite inquiry would have gotten them a simple, polite response.

It was true they were in strange woodlands and possibly enemy territory, but it wasn't very likely they would get where they were going without daring to ask where they were.

The crude maps they had been given were useless. Following them precisely had led them to the edge of a very steep cliff, and the implication might have been clear to Elizabet if she wasn't so certain her father had sent them on this journey for their betterment and not to their demise.

His new wife, on the other hand, Elizabet wasn't so certain of. Were dear Margaret to have her way, all of her father's children would drop from her sight forever. And just to be certain Elizabet and John were the first to go and stay gone, she had sent her brother, Tomas, along to see the task done. She had insisted vehemently that Tomas accompany their party, and Elizabet was certain Margaret had done so to be sure that Elizabet and John would be safely out of her way. It had been made clear to Elizabet that Margaret did not want them in her home.

Elizabet didn't like her.

There was something about her demeanor that seemed a bit deceitful. Why her father seemed so blind to it Elizabet didn't know. Margaret was beautiful, to be sure, but her eyes lacked any warmth at all—though her father was old, and Elizabet supposed he was grateful enough to have a wife so young no matter that she might be a shrew.

Men were silly creatures.

Sweet Jesu, but she didn't want one. If Piers were kind enough, he'd simply allow her to keep her dowry and spare her the misery of finding her a husband.

These men who traveled with her were a perfect example of male stupidity.

Of the four sent to escort them, all were of fairly equal standing, and none seemed the least inclined to follow the other. Not even Tomas seemed able to quell their bickering. If her brother John had been a bit older and perhaps more confident in himself, he might have taken matters into his own hands and dared to make his own decisions. As it was, they were each intent on following his own direction, and John was helpless to lead them.

It was no wonder they were lost.

God's truth, Elizabet had nearly had her fill of them all. She was tempted to seize John's sword from his scabbard and force them to follow her. She was unaccustomed to standing meekly aside while men bickered amongst themselves like old women. The men her mother had known had been strong men of stature, accustomed to giving orders, but her mother, in her own way, had been as strong as they. She had been well educated, intelligent and full of mettle. As a result, Elizabet had little patience for feeble people.

Where were those bickering fools anyway?

She rose, brushing herself off. They had all dashed into the woods to relieve themselves, her brother John with them, and the dog had gone missing behind them.

None, as yet, had returned, and Elizabet was growing impatient with the wait.

"Harpy!" she called out, wanting the comfort of her dog's presence. She didn't particularly like it much that Harpy had practically attached herself to John. Harpy was a finicky animal! It was her dog, not his. She loathed to be petty about the matter, but it was the only thing she had left of her mother, aside from the crucifix she wore on her girdle.

She started into the woods, calling for the wayward dog. Though Elizabet could hear the men's voices nearby, she couldn't see them. If Harpy were with them, Elizabet reasoned, the dog must surely have heard her calling by now. She must have wandered farther away, she reasoned, and if Elizabet waited for those babbling men to return before setting out to search for her, she'd be halfway back to England before they found her. Elizabet called the dog again, praying she wouldn't stumble upon the men at their business.

"She's not here!" shouted John from the bushes ahead, and Elizabet turned at once to avoid them.

"I'm going to look for her," she told him, grateful that he had spoken up so that she wouldn't barrel through the bushes and embarrass herself.

"Don't wander far, Liza!" John cautioned her.

"I won't!" she assured him and smiled at his show of concern.

Poor John.

Mayhap she worried overmuch about him, but he seemed so fragile at times. His wit was sound and quick, though his frail body failed him far too oft. The youngest of her father's legitimate children, he seemed ever ready to do battle over the least little thing. It was as though he had always something to prove, and Elizabet finally understood why.

His fears had finally been realized.

Like Elizabet, he had been too easily discarded.

She had grown to love him, though she hadn't known him very long. He was the one person who had welcomed her without reservation when first she'd arrived at her father's house—

not that the others had treated her poorly, they had simply never embraced her.

And still, despite the other children holding her somewhat apart, she had thought she'd found a safe haven after so many years of having no family and no place to call her own. And then her father had gone and wed that horrid woman, and Elizabet had been put out within a fortnight of their wedding.

But she refused to allow herself to wallow in self-pity. This was her opportunity at last. Unlike her mother, she would not be shackled to some man, dependent upon his good graces to feed her and her children. Nay, and moreover, she would have no children and no man to keep her. Here in the wilds of Scotia she would be free to live as she chose, unencumbered by the fetters of matrimony. She would beg Piers to return her dowry to her, and she would find a way to care for herself.

She was determined to make the best of the remainder of her life.

And it wasn't as though anyone would have her anyway. She had nothing to bring to any marriage aside from her body and her mind. Her meager dowry hadn't even been enough for her father to keep her.

She had been taught young where men placed their value. A woman's worth was determined by two things. The first and most important was

what they could bring a man by way of riches
and heirs. The second was what they could do
in bed to bring him pleasure, and the latter
would gain her no more than it had her mother.

Her poor mother had worked hard for every
morsel of food the two of them had placed in
their mouths, and in the end she had died alone.
And her father's wife, she who had borne him
five children and had given him her dowry, had
lost her husband's heart to some woman whose
body had brought him greater joy.

In either case, it was a matter of one man's
satisfaction and some poor woman's unappre-
ciated labors.

Well, mayhap her father's new wife would
reap all the rewards her mother and his first wife
never received.

It all seemed so unfair.

But there was no time for sorrow or regret.

Her mother had been dead now three years,
and she must be responsible for her own well-
being. And as God was her witness, the first
thing she intended to do after she found Harpy
was go back and speak to that old woman in the
little hut. She bloody well hoped by the time she
returned the men would be ready to listen to reason. There could be little harm in simply talking
to the old woman. Once she realized who their
father's cousin was, she was like to greet them
courteously. Piers de Montgomerie was, after all,

her neighbor. But it really didn't matter to Elizabet whether those accursed men approved or not, because if they refused to go back to beg for directions, Elizabet would simply go alone—fie on them!

If there was one thing she truly regretted she'd not inherited of her courtesan mother it was the cunning and smoothness of tongue to control such hard-headed, self-important men. She had witnessed on a thousand occasions how painless it was for women born with such gifts to gain their hearts' desire. But Elizabet was not fortunate enough to be one of their breed. She had little guile and didn't have much patience with women who did, if the truth be known. Still, there was something to be said for diplomacy, as her dear mother had never gone without whereas here she was struggling to get by with no home to speak of and no future within sight.

To put it precisely, she was aimlessly wandering these woodlands with four men who didn't seem to be able to follow the nose on their face, seeking a distant family member she had never met—who probably had no inkling she even existed. For all she knew, Piers might turn them away the instant they found him. Why, after all, would he wish to be burdened with the bastard child of a cousin he wasn't the least obliged to?

Her life had gone to the bloody dogs.

And speaking of which . . . She studied the forest for some sign of Harpy.

Where the devil could she have gone?

It was getting late, and the woods were beginning to darken. The bright greens had turned to grays, and fireflies had begun to twinkle before her eyes.

"Harpy!" she called out again, and suddenly she heard an answering bark in the distance. "There you are!" she exclaimed, relief flooding through her. She began to run. She didn't know what she'd do without that silly, cantankerous dog!

She followed the sound of barking, only to freeze, startled by what she discovered.

Chapter 3

He was by far the biggest man she'd ever feasted her eyes upon—a behemoth if Elizabet had ever spied one. But his tone as he spoke to Harpy was gentle. He knelt at a distance, coaxing Harpy to come to him, and his size was evident even crouched upon his haunches.

"Here, doggy," he was saying, and he clapped his hands. "Come here, doggy!"

She swallowed her protest as she watched him, fascinated.

Deep golden hair framed a face that was almost too lovely for a man, and even in the twilight, she could clearly see the brilliant blue of his eyes, framed by thick, dark lashes.

Fireflies twinkled between them, giving Elizabet the dizziest sensation as she stared.

She had to remind herself to breathe.

And then he stood, and she nearly fell backward in shock over his height.

His height was monstrous!

And sweet Jesu, he was wearing the most barbarous garment! It appeared something like the ancient togas she'd seen depicted in the drawings in her mother's manuscripts, but with brilliant color. And his legs were bare, thick, muscular. His arms were bare, as well, as was most of his chest. And he wore an enormous sword in his scabbard.

"My God!" she whispered in awe and scrambled behind the nearest tree, though somehow, she didn't quite fear him. Something about his demeanor and the gentle look in his eyes set her at ease though perchance she shouldn't have been so trusting. She peered at him around the tree, her heart hammering. "Sweet Mary," she said low.

He must have heard her, because he glanced in her direction, searching.

And then he found her.

Their eyes met.

Whatever words Elizabet might have uttered in that moment were forgotten as she stared into his eyes. Mayhap she should have run, but she stayed as firmly rooted to the ground as the tree she now leaned on for support. Never in her life had she seen a man so big and beautiful and golden as the very sun.

"Who are ye?" he demanded of her.

She didn't answer.

She couldn't answer.

The two of them stared at each other, startled by the other's presence.

Though she was nearly hidden by the tree, Broc could see her face well enough to know he'd never seen her before. He knew almost everyone in these parts, save for those who had settled with Piers de Montgomerie. This woman was like no one he'd ever encountered.

"Who are you?" she demanded in return, and the haughty tone of her voice grated upon his nerves.

Dark hair, chiseled brows, and lips so full and red they appeared painted were his first impressions.

"I asked ye first, wench."

He found himself wishing she would come out so he could better see her. Only her head was visible peeking around the tree. Curiosity needled him.

"Why should I tell you?" she argued.

Because he wanted to know where to find her again should he scare her away.

"Because . . . We Scots dinna take to strangers in our home."

"Your home?"

English by the sound of her voice, but what was she doing in these parts alone? He glanced about for some sign of her companions, but the woods were empty save for the woman, her mangy dog and Broc.

She came out from behind the tree at last, looking more contrary than she had a right to look. "I am hardly in your home!" she argued.

"This land is my home," he assured her. "Every tree in this woodland is mine and my brother's. Every leaf you spy upon the ground belongs to my kinsmen!"

She cocked her head as though in censure. "Possessive family you have!"

Saucy wench.

"Well"—she stood straight, hands upon her hips—"you might tell your brother when you see him that it is far more blessed to share."

The wench was taking him far too literally. "I dinna have a brother, woman."

"Nay?" She lifted her brows. "Then perhaps you should have listened to your mother when she advised you not to lie."

She dared scold him?

"Och, wench, I dinna have a mother, either," he said more sullenly than he'd intended to. But she appeared more offended than compassionate at his declaration.

"Of course you do! Everyone has a mother!"

"Aye, well, mine is dead," he replied sharply, hoping to shut her up. The subject remained a painful one even after all these years. And this wench was beginning to grind his nerves. No woman had dared reprimand him since he'd been but a wee lad.

"So is mine!" she countered. "Though I would hardly say I had no mother! Ungrateful behemoth!"

Startled by her obvious rancor, Broc merely stared at her. Only Page FitzSimon had ever dared speak to him so impudently—not since first meeting his laird's wife had he met a tongue so unruly.

Behemoth?

She'd called him a bloody behemoth!

He nearly laughed out loud at the absurdity of it all. She was hardly small for a woman, but neither was she any match for any man—and yet she stood, antagonizing him as no man had ever dared.

"Who are ye?" he demanded of her.

"A substitute for your manners, since you seem not to have any!" she countered.

He resisted the urge to walk over and toss her over his knee.

Foolish wench. What if he were, in truth, some ruffian? She would lose more than her impudent tongue. She must not be alone in these woods, or she would never dare speak to him so brazenly.

"Did no one ever warn ye to mind yourself before strangers, woman? If ye dinna hush, I will find a better use for that tongue."

He'd never threatened a woman before, but he'd damned sure like to kiss that mouth—and not tenderly at all.

English vixen!

"That is *my* dog," she informed him baldly, evidently disregarding his threat, and the animal, as though it understood, turned to face her, though it didn't move. "Come here, Harpy!" she called.

Harpy sat stubbornly.

Broc quelled his laughter.

In the mood he was in, he nearly called the dog just to spite her. He'd always had a way with animals, and he had no doubt the dog would come to him, particularly if he patted the pouch at his waist, tempting it with more food. She was obviously starving the poor beast to death and didn't deserve the bloody dog anyway.

"And just who are ye?" he asked again, more firmly this time.

Little good it did him.

"Who I am is none of your concern!"

Beautiful little shrew.

He'd definitely enjoy kissing those full lips. His body hardened slightly at the thought.

"I'd beware," he cautioned her. "I'd say 'tis long past time for wee lassies to be abed."

She'd better run home if she knew what was good for her. His patience was nearing its end.

She came completely out from her hiding place and slapped her leg, calling the dog irately. "I am hardly a wee lassie!" she argued.

Broc could see that clearly enough.

His brows lifted as his eyes were drawn to her ample breasts. They strained at the bodice of the lavish ruby gown she wore, teasing him. "All the more reason not to be wandering strange woodland at twilight," he advised her darkly, feasting his eyes upon her sweet bosom. She was blessed in a way few women were, with full, luscious breasts and a tiny waist that was well emphasized by the golden girdle that hung low on her hips. God's truth, a woman like that could make a man forget his manners.

"Come here, Harpy!" she commanded the animal, her tone unyielding.

But the dog remained, peering up at Broc and wagging its tail amiably.

Good dog, he thought a little smugly. "You realize not all ghouls prey on wee lassies," he advised her, his loins tightening as he watched her approach the animal. "Some prefer their women grown."

"Oh?" She hesitated at his threat, stopping, but belied the gesture by raising her chin with a defiance he knew she couldn't possibly feel—not if she had half a wit about her. "Do they?" she asked a little too haughtily and lifted those beautiful breasts as though to taunt him. Her nipples jutted high against the velvety material, and he wondered if her aureoles were dark or light and whether she were maiden or married.

She looked a little like a courtesan, he mused, richly adorned to attract her pigeon. Only once had he chanced to see a woman like her—when he and Iain had met with King David at one of their sovereign's English fiefs.

Something about her eyes, however, seemed far more innocent than her dress proclaimed.

He nodded. " 'Tis true," he said, and his blood began to simmer as he watched her watching him. His mood shifted, and he experienced in that instant a lustfulness such as he'd never known in all his days.

No woman had ever made him burn so easily.

"And which do you prefer?"

Suddenly he didn't feel the least bit charitable. He ought to teach the wench a bloody lesson, never mind who she was.

He narrowed his eyes. "Women, children, helpless little dogs. It matters not, I eat them all."

She blinked, as though misbelieving what he'd said, and he tried not to laugh at her expression, the way she cocked her head so uncertainly.

"I don't believe you!" she stated emphatically.

"Now, why would I lie to ye?"

"To frighten me, of course!"

God's teeth, if she had any sense at all, she would, indeed, be frightened. The growing strength of his desire was beginning to frighten him as well. "Is it working?"

"Nay!" she exclaimed with far too much self-assurance.

"Are ye certain?"

She crossed her arms. "Do I seem afeared to you?"

Not nearly enough.

The tension in his body was palpable. Broc had the sudden desire to toss her over his shoulder and carry her home, but he wasn't the barbarian she evidently thought him.

Still, he couldn't help himself.

He lunged at the dog. The animal yelped and bolted closer to its mistress. And he laughed. Meager thrill though it might be, it took the edge off his unwanted ardor.

The woman rushed to her pet to protect it, falling to her knees and hugging its neck, completely disregarding any threat to herself. "You wouldn't dare!"

Silly woman.

He frowned at her response. "Didn't anyone ever tell ye never to confront a scoundrel? That dog can take care of himself, woman. You, on the other hand, should have run."

She lifted her chin, glaring at him. "A poor scoundrel you make. Do you always scold your victims when they play into your hands?"

He arched a brow. "Is that what you are doing? Playing into my hands?"

She hugged her dog protectively. "Hardly!"

"And you aren't the slightest bit afeared?"

She lifted that lovely chin a notch higher. "Not at all."

He feigned another charge at her, and she fell back, shrieking in alarm.

Broc laughed, satisfied with her reaction.

The dog began to snarl at him.

Well, he hadn't wanted the damned dog anyway. It was just another mouth to feed, another body to worry about. He damned well should have learned his lesson after Merry!

He couldn't help but smile over the way the woman scurried to her knees, shielding the animal with that delightful body. She quieted the beast at once, cooing to it softly. She had long, beautiful legs. He'd gotten a generous glimpse of their length and her perfectly round bottom as she'd fallen backward onto her rump.

She hugged the animal, not seeming to care that her knees were soaking up muck from the forest floor. Her long, dark hair was bound in a single thick braid generously woven with luminous golden ribbons, though the style was thoroughly ruined by the wayward curls that escaped confinement and framed her lovely face.

And she was lovely, indeed.

"You are a churlish man!" she accused him.

"So I've been told," he said without the least remorse.

"Have you no couth at all?" Her eyes flashed at him with disdain. She loosened her grip on the animal now it had calmed.

Broc shrugged, trying not to chuckle at her show of fearlessness. "Dinna ye know we Scots are all ruthless barbarians?"

She straightened her spine a bit at that.

" 'Tis true. We eat our bairns when they arena born strong enough and use whole trees for toothpicks after."

" 'Tis nonsense!" she exclaimed, with more confidence than he thought she felt. She frowned beautifully. "Though I *have* heard you toss trees at each other in silly contests to prove your manhood!"

Broc lifted a brow at her reply. "Did ye, now?"

She was a delightful contradiction, this woman. Dressed as befitted a queen and yet kneeling in the muck like a beggar beside her dog, hair mussed, eyes glittering with the spirit of a warrior.

He almost wished she weren't a bloody Sassenach.

Though his days of loathing the English simply because of their birth were long gone, he placed about as much trust in them as he did Page's bastard da. His laird's wife's father was the epitome of those he'd come to despise, those who had murdered his parents and changed the course of his life forever. Because of Page, he no longer heard that distinctive accent and saw black rage, but neither did he feel completely at ease in their presence.

This woman was no exception.

Where one was, there were likely to be more, and he scowled at that thought. They were like vermin, traveling together in packs.

"What are you staring at?" she hissed at him.

Feeling suddenly wary, Broc ignored her question and turned to study the woods from whence she'd appeared. His neck prickled as he examined their surroundings.

His warrior's intuition told him there was someone there . . . in the woods . . . watching . . .

He spied the man almost at once, nearly hidden by a cluster of thick oaks.

It was an Englishman, no doubt, by the manner of his dress. He was standing, bow in hand, ready to loose the arrow. At first Broc thought himself the quarry, but the man's train of thought was so fixed on his target that he had not even realized Broc had spied him.

He was after the woman.

The realization stunned Broc, and he stood there an instant too long.

The arrow flew.

Broc didn't think, only reacted. He hurled himself at the girl, knocking her backward.

Chapter 4

It happened too swiftly.

Harpy yelped and bolted away.

Elizabet screamed.

She'd felt safe with her father's men so near, but she had been a witless fool! He made no move to stop her, so she screamed louder until he unsheathed a dagger from his boot and she gulped in fear. He bounded to his feet, dragging her up with him, knife in hand, and scanned the woods.

Harpy, the damned dog, merely sat there.

"Do something, you walking flea feast!" she shouted at the dog.

When it was clear she wasn't getting help from that quarter, she began once more to scream, until she realized that though his grasp was firm upon her sleeve, his attention was not on her.

"Let go of me!" she shouted, trying to see what held his gaze. He gripped her tighter, jerking her toward him. "What are you doing?" she demanded of him. "Let go of me!"

"Shut up!" he snapped.

"No!" Elizabet screamed louder than before. "I'm not alone!" she warned him.

"So I noticed," he replied.

He'd noticed? Elizabet struggled against his unyielding grip, trying in vain to free herself. "What are you talking about? I said let go of me!"

He was glaring into the woods as though expecting someone to come.

"Aye!" she warned him, glad he'd taken her threat to heart. "They'll be here any instant, so you'd better set me free!"

No matter how she fought, he was unshakable, unrelenting. Elizabet set loose a string of epithets.

He swung her about to face him suddenly, glaring at her. "Who are ye?" he demanded once more. "And who the hell is that bowman in the woods?"

"I don't have the first inkling what you are speaking of! What bowman? I saw no bowman!" It was very likely her brother and father's men come to rescue her, but she wasn't about to say so.

Let him worry!

He shook her roughly. "Who are ye, woman?"

"Ouch! You're hurting me!"

"Not as much as that bloody bowman intended to!"

He was speaking nonsense.

"Elizabet!" her brother John shouted from a distance.

"John!" she yelled back.

She wanted to warn him to get help. Her brother was no match for this Scots barbarian, but the behemoth jerked her against his chest and slapped a hand against her mouth, holding her fast.

Jesu, he was smothering her!

Elizabet bit his thumb.

He yelped in pain but didn't release her.

She bit harder, and he pressed the knife to her throat.

"Let go!" he threatened her, "or I'll leave you to their mercy!"

What the devil was he talking about? Leave her to their mercy?

Elizabet refused, biting down harder until she tasted his blood.

He exploded with a profusion of oaths that would normally have made her blush. "Fool woman!"

In that instant came a shout unlike any Elizabet had ever heard before. Her brother came first through the trees, his eyes bulging, charging at them as though he would bowl them over. He was bellowing hideously, and Elizabet could scarce tell whether it was in anger or fear. Mayhap both.

"Release her, Scots bastard!" John shouted at them.

She released the man's thumb long enough to scream her brother's name. "John, nay!" she shouted, and tried again to warn him to go get help, but the Scot cast her roughly away, switching his dagger to his injured left hand and unsheathing his sword with his right, wielding it in a movement so swift she scarce believed her eyes.

The most ungodly sound spewed from his lips as John attacked him. The Scot swung his weapon, felling him with very little effort.

The battle was over before it had begun.

"John!" Elizabet screamed, and rushed toward her brother's unconscious body. She didn't care if the devil Scotsman was standing over him. Too late, she could hear shouts from her father's men as they neared. Sobbing, she fell to her knees beside John, pushing the Scot away.

"Leave him alone!" she demanded. "John!" she cried out, turning to assess his injuries. He was sprawled on the bracken, but there wasn't any visible blood. Still, his face was pale, and his lips were already turning blue. He lay as still as a cadaver. "Look what you've done!" she screamed up at the Scot, tears pricking her eyes.

Her father's men rushed into the clearing, but Elizabet didn't look up. Where the hell had they been when she'd needed them? She held John's face, begging him to wake. He was the only family she truly had left—her only friend! "John!" she cried softly, but he didn't move.

"You've killed him!" she screamed at the Scot, and looked up in time to see him hurl his dagger into one of her father's men. Wide-eyed, the man fell backward, the knife protruding from his breast. The other two came to a halt and froze.

Where the bloody hell was Tomas?

Elizabet scanned the woodland, her heart hammering as she searched for his face, desperate for his aid. John had fallen, so had Edmund, and the two remaining, she feared, were not enough to overpower this madman.

They stood staring at one another, at an impasse, her father's men unwilling to approach. Only one of the two remaining was even armed.

Without warning, the Scot jerked her up, dragging her backward. Once more he pressed his blade to her throat. "Dinna move," he hissed at her. "Stay back!" he warned her father's men. "Or she dies!"

Neither stepped forward to help her.

Jesu, she didn't know whether to be grateful or incensed.

Swallowing, torn between fear and grief, she

allowed the Scotsman to drag her backward into
the woodland.

How could she have endangered them all so
frivolously?

"Release her at once!" a voice demanded.

Broc pressed his blade more firmly against the
woman's throat in warning.

"Ye must think I'm brainless," he answered.
He dragged her backward with him, forcing her
into the woods. He did not intend to hurt her,
but he had no wish for her companions to know
it. Their livery was the same as that of the bowman he had spied in the woods, but that man's
face was not among these who had come to save
her.

Or had they come to kill her?

She seemed to know them, and yet there was
no mistaking the fact that one of their party had
only moments before tried to murder her. The
arrow had missed them both, embedding itself
in a tree behind her, but it hadn't been aimed at
him, of a certain, and he didn't have time to
make explanations to the she-wolf howling in his
ear.

He could bloody well leave her, aye, but what
would come of her then?

Did these men intend to harm her?

Did they have any idea that one of their own
had tried to kill her?

If he left her to their mercy, would he be signing her death warrant?

Somehow, it mattered to him what happened to her.

And who the hell was John?

Her lover?

She certainly seemed distraught enough over his slight wound. Broc had scarce grazed him with the butt of his dagger. The idiot Sassenach must have swooned!

A thousand questions barreled through his mind, but there was no time to mull any of them over. He made a swift decision, relying on his instinct to guide him. It rarely led him astray.

He drew the girl back with him away from the two men. "If either of ye follow," he warned them, "I'll slice her throat before your eyes!" And in case that wasn't deterrent enough, he added, "And then I'll cut your hearts from your worthless Sassenach bodies and feed them to the dogs!"

He watched as they both at once turned to look at the man he'd felled, considering his threats. Evidently deciding he was capable of doing exactly what he threatened, neither of them moved to disobey him.

Bloody cowards, both of them!

Were this his own mistress, he would have given his life to protect her.

He placed a hand over her mouth. "Trust me,"

he whispered in her ear, trying to calm her.

She rewarded him with a kick in the shin.

"Ouch!"

Ungrateful wench!

He pressed his blade to her neck, silencing her, realizing that she couldn't possibly understand he was only trying to help her. He didn't have time to try to convince her. Brute force was the fastest way to gain her compliance.

Slowly, until he was out of the Sassenachs' sight, he pulled her backward into the forest, and then, once they could no longer be seen, he seized her by the arm, holding her firmly, and dragged her behind him.

He hoped she wouldn't give him too damned much trouble. He was doing this for her own good. "You'll keep your mouth shut if ye know what's good for ye!" he told her.

"You killed my brother!" she accused him, struggling to free herself. "Stop! I have to go back!"

A sense of relief washed over him. It was her brother he'd felled, not her lover. Somehow, that knowledge pleased him.

"You're not going back!" he assured her, jerking her arm, though not to hurt her. "Your brother isna dead, lass!"

"I saw you swing at him!" she argued, and dug in her heels, resisting. "I'm not going with you! You can't make me! Do you have any notion who I am?"

"If I did, wench, d'ye think I'd have asked ye three times to tell me?"

She kicked him again and fell upon her rump, fighting harder to free herself.

"My father will kill you for this!" she hissed up at him, struggling valiantly.

Be damned, if he needed this trouble. It had started out to be a damned fine day. Why did he have to go and befriend her stupid dog?

"He would have to catch me first, lass."

And they would if he remained an instant longer. Muttering an oath, he swung her to him, tossing her over his shoulder, stifling her protests. She gasped, and he knew he'd knocked the breath from her. Good, mayhap it would silence her long enough to get them safely away.

He knew these woods better than any but Seana. There was no way her men would catch him, even with his pretty little burden, not once he was on his way.

"Trust me!" he bade her, knowing it was a ridiculous request considering the circumstances. Tossing her over his shoulder, he ran deeper into the forest.

"Trust you!" she exclaimed, when she caught her breath. She pounded his back furiously with her dainty fists. "Let me go, you Scots barbarian! Crude man!"

Broc didn't give her a choice.

She was going to have to trust him.

Instinct told him he was doing the right thing. Whether they were all in league, or not, he knew without doubt someone in her party wanted her dead. Perhaps they all did, for all he knew. Once he reached Seana's old, abandoned home, he would settle her down and simply explain. She'd thank him then.

He'd very likely saved her life.

As for her brother, someone else would nurse his headache, because he was no more dead than his sister was timid.

Tomas waited for his companions to leave and then came from his hiding place among the trees.

They would go after the mounts first, he knew, and then ride after Elizabet.

He went quickly to Edmund's body to see if he still lived and finding him dead, he smiled in satisfaction. His task would go all the easier now. The last thing he wished was for Edmund to witness what he must do next. He was the only one Tomas might have to worry about. The other two were stupid fools who were easily impressionable. If he told them the Scots idiot had sliced John's throat, they would believe it. And if they didn't, he would make it worth their while to keep their stupid mouths shut.

He hurried, then, to where John lay and saw

that the milksop still breathed. He turned John's head, searching for a wound, and found nought but a graze at his temple. Damned wench was what he was! The man didn't deserve to live.

He peered at John in disgust.

If Tomas allowed it, every cent of Margaret's money would end in the bellies of her husband's children, and Elizabet, his bastard daughter, would place her dowry in de Montgomerie's purse. But he wasn't going to allow it. And Elizabet's purse would be an added reward for protecting Margaret's interests.

He was certain Margaret had never intended for these two embarrassments to reach their destination. Every one of the old man's children was a burden upon his stepsister's coffers. But until now, he'd failed in every attempt to eliminate these two leeches, and he was growing vexed. Every time he'd thought himself at an advantage, Edmund had managed to foil him.

He peered back at Edmund's body.

The fool would no longer trouble him. The Scotsman had seen to that well enough. His aim had been deadly and true. And now, thanks again to the Scot, he had witnesses who would claim the man had murdered John, as well.

It couldn't be more perfect.

As for Elizabet . . . He glanced into the woods.

Her fate would be determined by the brigand who had stolen her. God's truth, the Scotsman could keep her or kill her, it mattered not which, just so that she never returned.

And to make certain, Tomas intended to remain in Scotia long enough to make sure the slut's daughter never returned. Her dowry was his now, every last jewel, every last coin. Her stupid bitch of a mother must have spread her legs for every man who had passed through Henry's court.

Tomas had even had her once, and if he recalled aright, she had charged him double what she'd charged his friend. Apparently, she hadn't liked him any more than her daughter seemed to, though she had been far too greedy to turn him away. Well, the joke was on her, because he was going to have his money back and then some!

His only regret was that he couldn't return to Margaret the golden crucifix Elizabet wore, the one he had so stupidly given her mother in an attempt to win her favors. More than that, he'd love to gift her with Elizabet's unruly tongue on a platter as proof of her demise.

Elizabet was a termagant if ever Tomas had known one, stubborn and defiant every moment she breathed. His sister had developed a particular dislike for her. Tomas had, as well. She had treated him with the cool disdain with which her whore of a mother had treated him—but he didn't have the least desire to bed Elizabet.

God's teeth, she was like to be no better than her mother was.

How dared she think herself too good for him? Her damned dowry was all she was good for.

As for the old man . . . He wouldn't live forever, and though his seed had been fruitful and he had multiplied his heirs, neither were they invulnerable, not a one of them. One by one they would find their own demise, and in the end it would be Tomas and Margaret once more.

Just the two of them.

John stirred, moaning, and Tomas unsheathed his knife to be ready, anger surging through him.

No one would stand in his way.

The youth opened his eyes, looking dazed for an instant, and then comprehension seemed to dawn as he spied Tomas with the knife.

"Elizabet!" he rasped, and tried to rise.

Tomas slammed his head back on the ground. John's eyes crossed at the force of the impact. With a hand at his forehead, Tomas held the youth down firmly and smiled at him.

He waited until awareness returned to his expression.

"She's dead," he said with relish, and savored John's reaction.

"Nay," the boy croaked, horror entering his eyes. He swallowed, and Tomas watched the bob of his throat with great attention.

Tomas despised the way Elizabet seemed to

coddle him at every turn, putting him before everyone, though the fool could not have led a buzzard to a bloody carcass.

It amazed him. The cretin didn't appear afraid, though he damned well should have been.

But he couldn't know Tomas's intent.

"Ahh, Christ!" he sobbed. "Are ye certain, Tomas?"

So he loved her, the moron.

Too bad.

He might have been one who would understand and not condemn Tomas's affections for Margaret. "Aye," he replied with a keen sense of victory. "And so are you."

And having said that, he sliced the blade across John's throat as swiftly as the serpent strikes and then hurriedly cut the bulging leather pouch from his belt.

That done, he stepped away to await the others' return.

He couldn't be more pleased with the turn of events.

Chapter 5

"I'm going to scream!"

"Like ye havena already?" Broc said.

She whacked him on the bare back for his flippant response. It stung like a whoreson's mother, but he didn't give her the satisfaction of yelping.

"And I'm going to keep screaming until we're found!" his twisting burden assured him.

"Och, lass," he answered calmly, "my ears would thank ye no' to."

Her answering shriek nearly pierced Broc's ears.

Vixen!

He managed to ignore that, as well, though his teeth hummed at the shrill sound of it. He was feeling generous. They were near their destination with no sign of her companions' pursuit, so she could scream all she wanted to.

Seana's abandoned home, the one she'd shared with her drunkard father, was hidden so deep within the woodland and was so completely in union with its natural environment that he doubted anyone would discover them. It would be safe enough to keep her there until he had assessed the situation better.

She was lean, not so lean that he could see her bones, but he could damned well feel them as she squirmed over his shoulder. Her fists continued to pound his back in protest.

Getting desperate, she pressed her teeth into his shoulder, and Broc squeezed her leg—painfully, he knew.

"That wouldna be a verra good idea, lass," he advised her, gripping her right thigh more firmly still.

He'd be damned if she was going to take a chunk out of him so easily.

"I don't much care what you think is a good idea!" she countered, but she didn't bite him, and he loosened his grip upon her leg as a reward. "Where are you taking me?" she demanded haughtily.

"Somewhere safe," he assured her.

"Safe! Hah!" she shrieked. "The only safe place is someplace far from you!"

And then her mettle seemed to falter, because he heard her breath catch. "Oh, God, John," she cried out, and went suddenly limp over his shoulder.

She started to cry.

He was glad she had finally stopped battling him, but he felt guilt-stricken that she was so worried for her brother.

"The worst he will suffer is a headache," he reassured her.

The brother had swooned, else Broc had managed to hit him just so to knock him out, no more. In either case, Broc knew of a certain the lad was still breathing when they left him. His sister had simply been too distraught to notice.

"But I saw you swing at him!" she persisted.

"You saw me hit him with the butt of my dagger," he corrected her.

They reached Seana's abandoned home, and he set her down before the door. It took her a moment to regain her footing.

"We're here, lass," he said.

"How wonderful!" she replied, her tone somewhere between anger and fear. Broc recognized both in her voice, and he admired her for standing up to him. She was nought like her milksop brother. No swooning miss did he have on his hands. In truth, she had more courage than most men.

Her dark brows collided as she considered whether to believe him. "You merely hit him with the butt of your dagger?"

Broc nodded, watching her expression.

Much of her hair had worked itself free from her thick braid and fallen in disarray about her face. He brushed it aside to reveal a pink nose, evidence of tears, and eyes so stark a green they seemed almost unreal.

She shrugged away from him, glaring at him accusingly.

"Ye have my word that your brother is going to be fine."

Her eyes glazed with unshed tears.

"Och, lass, dinna cry," he begged her. He reached out to wipe away the tears, unsettled to see them.

She slapped his hand away and averted her gaze.

He was glad she'd done that. God's teeth, if he'd peered into those eyes an instant longer, he might have never turned away. He wanted to tell her not to worry, that he wouldn't harm her, but his tongue was suddenly too thick to speak.

Already, in little more than a few months, the forest had begun to reclaim Seana's hovel. Colin had forbidden his bride to return to this place, where so much had happened to dispirit her.

He watched the wench keenly from the corner of his eye as he worked the door free of the vines that had begun to tangle themselves within the doorframe. Once the door was forced open, he gently pushed her within the cairn, but not before she managed to cast him a malevolent glance.

Broc could scarce blame her.

He would explain everything once they were safely within.

He followed her inside and closed the door behind them, casting the room into shadows, but he knew his way around well enough not to trip over anything—not that there was much to trip over. The place was nearly empty. It was dank and rotten-smelling, like some crypt where no body had been laid to rest in years. Seana's old man had lived the last of his life huddled in a cold, damp corner of the single-room dwelling.

Broc didn't understand how Seana had lived here so long. He understood even less why her da hadn't gotten off his lazy, drunken arse and built them a small but respectable hut somewhere in these woods instead of shacking up in the ruins of an old cairn.

But none of that was really any of his affair.

The old man was dead now, Seana was comfortable and deliriously happy with her new husband, and the cairn would make a good hiding place until Broc could best determine what to do with his feisty little bit of baggage.

He pulled her further into the room. "You cannot keep me here!" she hissed at him, jerking away from him as though his touch disgusted her.

He grasped her firmly, pulling her back. " 'Tis for your own good, lass."

Not until he discovered who the bowman was did he intend to release her. He didn't wish to have her death heaped upon his conscience now that he had chosen to intervene. Sassenach or not, she was a woman in need of his protection, and what sort of man would he be if he refused to give it?

His mother had needed him once long ago, and he'd failed her. He'd not throw away opportunities to redeem himself.

He led the girl to the chair and sat her down at the table, then knelt in front of her to explain the situation as calmly as he was able.

Before he could open his mouth, she flew at him.

He caught her hands before she could do any damage and jerked her down once more.

"Stop! Listen to me."

"This place smells like death!"

"Aye, it does," Broc agreed. "Listen to me," he commanded once more, trying to calm her.

"Someone *will* find us!" She sounded hopeful. And angry. "And when they do, you will regret ever having laid a hand upon me, Scot!"

"Nay." He shook his head. "Trust me, lass, you will be safe here." Even those who had known Seana lived here had not been able to find the place even with precise directions. The dwell-

ing was well hidden between cliffside and woodland.

As soon as he was able to do so he would get
her some light. The place didn't look quite so
frightening with torches lit against the night.

"My men *will* find us!" she assured him,
sounding a little less certain.

Not unless they chose to be found.

"And if they cannot, my father will send more
men to aid the search! They *will* find me!"

He wanted to tell her that there would be no
need, if only she would listen to him. "They will
search in vain," he told her.

"My father's cousin will be furious!" she persisted. "He'll surely scour this land, and when
he finds me, he'll cut off your hands for daring
even to touch me!"

At least he was getting somewhere now.

"Tell me who your cousin is," he demanded.

Maybe her cousin would aid them. If he could
leave her in Seana's hovel, safe from the bowman, he could go and seek out her cousin.

"And what good would it do for me to tell you
who my cousin is? Will you set me free once you
know? Or will you then hold me for ransom?"

She struggled to free her hands from his grip,
but to no avail. He held her fast.

"Ransom?"

The thought hadn't even occurred to him.

"That thing you do when you abduct innocent

people to extort money from unsuspecting victims!" she explained acidly. "Don't tell me the thought never crossed your mind, Scot!"

He blinked and stared up at her and then grinned suddenly.

"Don't look at me that way!"

"Which way?"

"As though the thought only just occurred to you."

"Och, lass, well, how much are ye worth?"

She gasped in outrage.

Elizabet wanted to tell him that no one would pay ransom for her. She doubted a distant cousin who had no inkling she even existed and didn't have the first notion she was to be tossed at him like so much baggage would bother to lift a finger to help her. Nor could she fault him for it. And she wasn't about to give up her meager dowry, when it was all she had left in the world. Besides, even if she promised her captor every coin of it, she had no assurance that he would set her free. If this madman wished to ravage her, kill her and toss her body to the wolves, no one would care.

Then again . . . She peered about the room with no small measure of disgust. He really needn't even move her. She would rot here before anyone discovered her body.

He shook his head. "I dinna intend to ransom ye, wench."

Elizabet eyed him dubiously, unsure whether to be relieved or afraid at that revelation.

Her eyes adjusted to the dimness of the room, and she peered about, trying to gauge their surroundings. It *did* smell like death in this place. It reminded her of some old, forsaken crypt, like the ones her mother had spoken of in Spain where people moved the bones of loved ones to a common grave, and left them to litter the catacomb floors.

"What is this place?" she demanded to know.

"Someplace safe," he replied.

Light. She needed more light in order to be able to assess her chances of escape. "I'm afraid of the dark," she lied.

Or mayhap it wasn't a lie.

Somewhere near where she sat, the sound of little scurrying feet brought a gasp to her lips.

"If you'll behave," he told her, "I'll light a candle."

Elizabet bristled.

No one had commanded her to behave since she was a child. But she nodded anyway.

"I promise," she said grudgingly, and took comfort in the fact that a lie told in self-defense wasn't any sort of lie at all. God would surely never hold it against her.

The first opportunity this madman gave her to run she intended to use. But he stood between her and the door, giving her no chance, and she cursed him beneath her breath. She could see his silhouette move through the deepening shadows like some sinister wraith larger than life.

After an interminable time, the promised light appeared.

Elizabet blinked as she stared at the half-burned taper he held in his hand. Her gaze moved to his face, and again she blinked.

The bloody rotten devil had the face of an angel.

Not all angels were heavenly, she reminded herself. Lucifer was said to be the most beautiful angel of all.

At least with the candle lit, the room didn't appear nearly so sinister. It had obviously been used, though not recently, as someone's home. It was dusty now, and cobwebs had grown in the corners. Anything that might have made the place seem cozy had been removed, and all that remained were the barest essentials.

She was seated at a small, crude table, with a portion of its top lopped off. In one corner of the room was a small brazier, and stacked beside it were a few pots and pans. In another corner lay a lone pallet.

He went to the brazier, lit it, and then came toward her once more, his presence inescapable. She cast a yearning glance at the door.

"What is this place?" she asked him again.

He towered before her, looking down at her, and Elizabet swallowed.

"A friend lived here, but she's wed now and moved."

A lover, Elizabet wondered?

She cast him a disgusted glance, one brow arched. No man ever befriended a woman save to acquire her assets, be it her wealth or her body.

"A *friend*?" she said dubiously.

"Aye," he replied. "A verra good friend."

"Hmph!"

Was this their secret meeting place, then?

Her home?

Had he abandoned her here to wither in the dark and cold?

She wrinkled her nose in absolute disgust. If so, these Scots had much to learn about wooing a woman! Her mother, at least, had been showered with luxuries and bathed in exotic perfumes.

She couldn't hold her tongue. "If *this* is all you offered the poor woman, 'tis no wonder she wed someone else!"

He had the audacity to chuckle at her imputation.

"She wasna my woman."

"All the worse!" Elizabet chastened him, offering a baleful glance for his shameless confession.

As if that fact should excuse him!

"Nay, lass," was all he said in his defense.

"Men are curs!" she told him. "All of you! You live to eat, sleep, fight like bratty children, and you cuckold your fellows without conscience!"

He frowned at her. "Och, lass, she's my best friend's wife."

Her contempt increased. "And since when did that ever stop any man?" She stood and railed at him. She was becoming outraged now, just thinking of the injustices her mother had suffered at the hands of men like him. "You take and you take and you take! And you bloody well think the whole world belongs to you, and it matters not what a woman's wishes are." She jabbed him in the chest. "You pass her from hand to hand, whispering promises and, all the while, you intend to honor not a single word!"

He started to speak again, but Elizabet was beside herself with the insult. He'd hurt her brother, seized her against her will, and now he dared to stand before her and speak so casually of using some woman he hadn't a right to!

"Sweet Mary! You are all alike! You ought to be ashamed of yourselves! How dare you think yourself above me simply because of your gender!"

"Ye misunderstand me, lass." He was growing vexed with her. She could tell by his harassed expression.

"Of course!" Elizabet exclaimed.

She didn't seem to be able to keep herself from baiting him, and that simple fact unsettled her. God only knew, she wasn't a stupid woman. It was hardly wise to rankle her captor. She knew nought about this man, but her instinct was confusing her. Somehow, though he appeared threatening—a bigger man she'd never met—she didn't feel threatened. Foolish conclusion after she'd witnessed the felling of her own brother. Still, she didn't seem to be able to hold her tongue.

"Simply because you are possessed of a proud cock does not mean you can leave it to crow in every barn!" She knew it was a shocking thing for a woman to say, but she didn't much care. Good manners were reserved for those one wished to impress. She hardly cared what he thought of her.

"Good Christ, woman!" His cheeks turned rosy. "Dinna ye ever hush?"

"Nay!" Elizabet assured him. "And when you kill me, I'll not die silently. I vow my screams will haunt you until the day you die!"

"I'm no' going to kill ye, wench."

Relief nearly choked her words. "You're not?"

"Nay!"

Well, he would surely ravage her at least.

She narrowed her eyes at him. "When you rape me, I shall scratch out your eyes from your pretty face!"

He stood there looking at her as though she were deranged, and then shook his head. "God's teeth, I'm no' going to rape ye either, woman!"

This time, Elizabet couldn't keep the surprise from her tone. "You're not?"

"Nay," he said with far too much certainty.

It occurred to her suddenly to be offended.

It was that something in his tone that provoked her. He sounded as though the very notion of touching her was abhorrent. Sweet Jesu! Here she sat noting his beautiful face and body despite the gravity of the situation and feeling ashamed for her attention, and he obviously hadn't returned the attraction.

What was wrong with her that he didn't want her?

What was wrong with her that she wanted him to want her?

God have mercy! It was not that she *wanted* him to want her precisely, but she didn't want him *not* to want her, either.

The words were out of her mouth before she could stop them.

"Why not?"

Chapter 6

For an instant, Broc didn't believe his ears.

He screwed up his face at her. "Why not what, wench?"

She seemed to think about her question a moment and then rephrased it. "Just what do you intend to do with me if you don't mean to ransom me, kill me or ravage me?"

Her question amused him, though it shouldn't have.

He tried not to laugh.

The shudder of her delicate shoulders alerted him that she was frightened, but she was hardly cowering before him this moment, and he couldn't help but respect her for standing up to him. She stood as though waiting for his explanation, and he had a sudden ridiculous notion to kiss her.

The realization took him aback.

When was the last time he had even thought about kissing a woman? When was the last time he had craved one? Other than a distant affection for Page, he damned well couldn't remember.

He stared at her, trying to deny the thought, but it had already escaped. And like a wild horse fled from a barn, it refused to return from whence it came.

He set the candle down upon the table and watched the play of its golden light upon her body. Like a goddess she stood before him, looking lovely as a summer morn, and he couldn't remember a woman ever looking so deliciously exotic, so purely feminine.

She was tall but lean with the most perfect curves he had ever imagined running his hands over—full breasts that beckoned to his palms, a tiny waist that made him want to test its girth with his fingers, full hips that teased a man's imagination, long legs that made him yearn to feel them wrapped about his neck.

His mouth went dry as he admired her.

He wondered idly what she tasted like.

Mayhap not so idly.

He tried to recall himself, but couldn't keep from imagining those sweet lips upon his own, soft and full. They were lips made for loving a man. He wondered what they would feel like upon his body.

Christ.

He pushed away his lustful thoughts, swallowing at the sudden thickness in his throat. Dutifully, he ignored the stirring in his loins.

"I tried to explain, lass, but ye wouldna listen."

She said nothing, merely cocked her head at him expectantly, and he assured her at once, "Your brother is fine. Ye have my word of honor on that."

He could tell that she wanted to believe him. Her eyes begged him.

"And I truly mean ye no harm."

Still she listened, though her expression was dubious, and he was grateful for the opportunity to explain. He wanted to help if he could. "I took ye only because I believed ye to be in danger."

She lifted her chin, challenging him. "Fie! I saw the way you looked at me!"

He tensed at her insinuation. "And how was that?"

For an instant, she didn't speak, merely glared at him.

"As though you wanted me, and do not deny it!"

Anger flashed through him. Mayhap because he had done nothing save try to help her and she dared to question his honor, or mayhap simply because she spoke the truth and was looking at him now as though he were beneath her.

He reached out before he could stop himself,

seizing her by the arm. He jerked her against him, glaring back into her face.

"And because I'm a bloody Scot I canna control myself, is that right?" He wanted her to feel the hardness of his body, wanted her to know that he had been this way from the instant he had spied her. He wanted her to understand how long he had managed to control himself.

Still she did not cower, though she gasped aloud at his barely restrained violence. "You are the one who pointed out you were a barbarian who ate children and used trees for toothpicks, not I!"

He pressed her more firmly against him, willing her to understand.

She arched one of her perfect brows. "I have never met any man who was willing to restrain himself in the face of temptation. Why should you be any different?"

The statement made him wonder just how many men she had tempted. Though why should he care if she'd bedded half of England? he asked himself. He didn't even know her.

And aye, why should he be any different?

Fury clouded his thinking. He drew her fully against him, seizing a kiss.

Elizabet struggled against his embrace, trying to free herself, to no avail. His strength was unyielding. His arms were a cage of steel. His mouth bruised hers, taking without giving, and her heart hammered like a ram against her ribs.

The more she struggled, the harder he kissed her, until her knees grew wobbly and gave beneath her. Only when she clung to him weakly did he end the assault upon her mouth. But he didn't release her, and she was almost grateful, because if he had, she would have crumpled to a helpless pile at his feet.

He left her breathless and without words even to protest his embrace.

"Is that what you expected of me?" he asked her.

Elizabet's heart beat too fiercely. Words still would not come. Confusion embraced her as surely as did his arms.

Why was she not more angered by the liberties he had taken? Why was her heart fluttering so wildly within her breast? Fear mayhap, but something else as well—if she would be honest with herself.

When he released her and stepped away, it wasn't entirely relief she felt. She wavered on her feet and took a single step back, reaching for the table for support as she stared at him.

"As God is my witness, I dinna intend to ransom ye, nor to kill ye! Neither do I intend to abuse ye!"

"You mean not anymore?"

It seemed his eyes gleamed with rancor. "Remember that I also released you," he advised her darkly. "And realize that if it were my intention to ravage you, I wouldn't be standing here trying to reason with you."

Somehow, she managed to find her aplomb. "What danger could I possibly face save from you? I traveled with my brother and my father's men. What reason could they possibly have to harm me?"

It was a fitting question. One she expected him to answer if she was to believe him.

"I canna say," he allowed, still glaring at her. "I know only this. I stood looking directly at that bowman, and he saw me not at all. His gaze was trained solely upon you. He cared not one whit about me."

"What bowman? I don't believe you! Why should I believe anything you say?"

"The one I tried to tell ye about, woman! You were his target. I have no reason to lie to ye!"

Elizabet straightened but said nothing. He made no further advances, and she had the terrible feeling he was telling her the truth.

Neither of them spoke for the longest moment, merely stared at each other. She studied him, trying to discern the truth.

The anger seemed to drain from him even as she watched. "I wanted only the opportunity to tell ye what I saw," he reasoned with her, his tone somewhat calmer. "If ye dinna believe me, ye can leave." He waved her to the door.

She lifted both her brows. "Truly?"

"Aye, but before ye go, remember that I made no move toward you in the forest, not until the bowman presented himself." To prove he meant what he said, he stepped out of her way, leaving the path clear to the door. "If I were you, I'd watch my back."

She couldn't quite believe her ears. For the longest moment, she didn't move, didn't seem to be able to lift her feet.

"What are ye waiting for?" he asked her. "You're free to go."

She merely stared at him.

He didn't owe her anything, Broc told himself. She wasn't his responsibility.

If she wished to leave, so be it. He wouldn't stop her. He couldn't make her accept his aid.

Except that someone *was* trying to kill her, and the only thing Broc knew for certain was that it wasn't him.

He hoped she would stay.

If she would let him, he would be her voice and shield her from harm.

She took a step toward the door and hesitated, though she didn't look at him.

He made no move to stop her, save to say, "I promise to help ye if ye choose to stay."

Still she hesitated, staring at the door. She peered over her shoulder at him, narrowing her eyes suspiciously.

Broc crossed his arms, letting her make up her own mind. He sensed her strength, her need to be in control. If he begged her to stay, she would go. If he tried to stop her, she would await an opportunity to escape. She must remain of her own accord.

Their gazes held.

She tilted him a strange look, one he couldn't quite decipher, and then turned around and started walking slowly toward the door.

He waited patiently.

She kept walking.

And then she halted abruptly and turned. "You truly do not intend to stop me?"

Broc shook his head. "I said what I wished to say. The rest is up to you."

She turned again and contemplated the door. She was very near it, and he'd yet to move. She took another step toward it.

"I know without doubt," he told her, "that someone is trying to kill ye."

She stopped and cast him a questioning look over her shoulder. "How do you know it was not you the bowman wished to kill?"

"Because the man's eyes never met my own—not once—though I stared directly at him. He was watching you and only you."

She screwed her face as though she could not believe him, as though she didn't wish to, but her gut was whispering the truth.

"And ye didna see it," he continued, "but his arrow did strike the tree you were standing near. In fact, had I not brought you down, he wouldna have missed. His aim was true."

She shook her head, struggling with his revelation. "I saw no arrow," she contended.

"Och, lass, I would have taken the time to show ye, if only I could have, but there wasn't time even to breathe. Your brother assailed me, and I made the best decision I knew to make."

She cast him a resentful glance. "My brother was defending me."

"As I would have, were you my blood," he assured her. His arms remained crossed, and he had still yet to move.

He could tell the instant she began to believe him, because her shoulders slumped, and she turned around, pondering his words.

"Sweet Jesu," she exclaimed, and she returned to the table and sat, looking confused. "I cannot fathom why he should wish me dead," she said low.

Elizabet tried to recall the incident more clearly.

Could this man possibly be speaking the truth?

They *had* been speaking together in a harmless manner. And truth to tell, at the time she hadn't felt the least bit threatened by his presence, only annoyed that he was trying to steal her dog.

Oh, Harpy!

"My dog!" she said with a gasp, springing up from the chair in alarm. She hadn't even thought about Harpy in all this time. "She'll be lost!"

"I'm certain they took care of her, lass, but I'll find out," he assured her. "I give ye my word. And I'll bring her to ye if I can."

Why was he being so nice to her?

Why did he care what happened to her?

She was so confused.

And growing more so by the instant.

She sat again, her thoughts muddled. Her gut said trust him, though she knew him not at all.

But how could she trust this man she had never set eyes upon before this day?

Her hand went to her mouth. How could she trust him when he had bruised her lips with his kiss?

He had also been willing to let her go.

Who was this bowman he spoke of?

She nibbled at her lip, contemplating the possibilities. It must be Tomas. Who else could it be but Tomas? He was the only one not present when John was felled.

She peered up at him, studying his expression, trying to read his thoughts. In truth, why should he lie to her? What had he to gain? And if he'd intended to ravage her, he would never have ended his kiss. Nor had he harmed her, in truth. He had stolen a kiss in anger and then had set her away from him. Her cheeks burned with the memory of his embrace. She had been keenly aware of his body's reaction to her. She wasn't so naive that she didn't understand how a man's desire manifested itself. She didn't dare even look at him while her thoughts were centered there.

He swore her brother was unharmed, and she had to believe him.

She *wanted* to believe him!

But why would Tomas wish to kill her? Her father couldn't possibly have anything to do with it. Had Tomas escorted her all this way only to murder her in cold blood?

Nothing made sense.

She wasn't close with her father, but he was a kind man who'd felt terribly that he had no means to support all his children. And he may not have loved Elizabet, precisely, but he cared about her, and he certainly seemed to love John.

He'd wed Margaret in order to fill his coffers with gold to replenish his estates, but still there had not been enough to support his youngest son and bastard daughter. Nor had her dowry been adequate to find her a suitable husband— not in England. As she remembered it, it had pained him deeply to send John away with her, and he had done so with tears in his eyes.

She could not conceive that her father would plan their murder.

Nay.

Margaret, then? But why? What reason could Margaret possibly have to want her dead? And in truth, her brother Tomas had been nothing but kind to her the entire journey.

Still, this man standing before her seemed to be telling her the truth—at least, the truth as he believed it. And something about the look in his eyes begged her to trust him.

"Tell me who your cousin is, and I will go and speak with him on your behalf."

The predicament left her reeling.

Jesu, but Piers had no idea they were even coming. They carried the letter from her father, begging Piers' support, along with them. And it stood to reason that if Piers didn't know they were coming, he couldn't possibly be the one to wish her harm. Then again, neither was he obligated to champion her.

Still, it seemed her best course of action was to go to Piers and ask for sanctuary.

She sat again, the enormity of the situation making her legs weak.

"Piers de Montgomerie," she confided, and peered up at him hopefully. She took a tremendous risk in trusting him, and she prayed to God he spoke the truth. Then again, she prayed he didn't.

How could she bear it if her own father meant to kill her?

She relayed to him the rest of the tale, explained everything that was pertinent, omitting her precise relationship to Piers. He didn't need to know that. Nor did he need to know that Piers did not know of her. By the time he had the opportunity to speak with Piers, hopefully John would have found him as well, and Piers would certainly know her father's hand. That was enough. The letter John carried would make clear the rest. She explained about the letter her father had written and named the men she'd traveled with, all the while praying she'd made the right decision in trusting this man.

He sat down before her, listening calmly, hardly speaking a word, only nodding as she gave him her account, and she sensed his sincerity.

"And ye have no inkling who might wish ye dead?" he asked her.

Blinking numbly, Elizabet shook her head. "None. These men were commanded by my father to see us to our destination."

"What about Tomas?"

Elizabet shrugged. "My guess is that he wished to see the task done, but I never sensed any animosity from him."

He nodded. "Well, lass, if ye will trust me and remain here, I swear I will go directly to Piers with all that you have told me."

Elizabet cringed. "You intend for me to stay here"—she scrunched her nose in disgust—"in this place?" It gave her the shudders. She looked about to find the shadows had grown deeper. Night had fallen. "Nay!" she exclaimed. "I will come with you!"

"You are safer here," he assured her. "There is light aplenty, and I can travel more quickly alone."

"I can run swiftly!" she persisted.

"Aye, but not more swiftly than a missile. I would not wish ye to find yourself a target of that bowman again. It is safer for you to remain here," he insisted. "No one will bother you here, and I promise to return at once with help."

Elizabet swallowed as she looked again into his face. His blue eyes were filled with such compassion that she knew in her heart he meant all he proclaimed.

Those blue eyes, as he looked at her, appeared like those of an angel. He was her guardian angel.

The very thought of it took her breath away.

God had sent her an angel.

"I will stay only if you will not lock me in."

He smiled warmly. "I didna intend to, lass. If ye will look," he charged her, "there is no lock on the door."

She would have liked simply to trust him, but good sense told her to check. She did and found that he spoke the truth.

She turned and narrowed her eyes at him. "And leave me unfettered as well."

He lifted his brow at her, seemingly amused by her dictates. To show her they were empty, he held up his hands. "I seem to have forgotten the chains," he said in an attempted jest.

She sighed heavily, feeling suddenly weary. "Very well, then," she relented. "I'll remain here on the understanding that if you do not return anon, I will leave here and go to Piers myself."

His brow furrowed. "I would not advise leaving, lass. These woods are not so peaceable as they seem, and the way is long and perilous from here."

"Nevertheless, I will only remain if I am free to leave," Elizabet persisted.

"There will be no one to stop ye."

It was true.

"Very well, then I'll stay."

With that settled between them, he stood and looked down at her a long moment. And then he reached out and brushed the hair from her face. "A more bonny lass I have never seen," he told her.

Elizabet's heart jolted at the unexpected compliment. Her cheeks warmed at the memory of his kiss. She had the most overwhelming urge to fly at him and beg him not to go. Confusion embraced her once more.

"Och," he continued, "I canna imagine who would harm a hair on that lovely head."

His hand lingered, not touching her, though

very near her face, and she lowered her gaze, torn.

His words both thrilled and disquieted her.

If she were to be honest with herself, she wasn't entirely offended by his advances. Though now his advances began, and that simple fact nettled her. Gratitude quickly turned to resentment. Men never did anything without promise of reward, and thinking he meant now to claim his, she readied herself to defy him.

Never had a man spoken so softly to her and not wanted something in return. If he chose to abandon her after she refused him, then so be it. She would find her own way to Piers.

"There is a blanket in the corner," he surprised her by saying. "The night will grow cold."

She looked up at him, swallowing the sour retort she had readied.

A gentle giant stood before her with a smile so warm it squeezed her heart.

"I shall return soon with Montgomerie," he promised her, and then simply left her seated at the crude little table without saying another word.

He never even looked back as he shut the door behind him.

Elizabet pursed her lips as she stared at the closed door, contemplating her dubious savior. The man confused her more than any she had ever met.

"Surely he wants something," she muttered to herself.

Later he would try to claim his prize, she decided. Later he would offend her—once he returned. She could not believe any man would be so selfless as to expect nothing for his trouble.

And yet, nothing was precisely what he would get—aside from her gratitude and a simple thank you very much.

Elizabet's affections were not for sale, and she didn't want a man in her life.

Freedom was too close at hand.

Chapter 7

❧❧❧❧

Broc might have guessed Montgomerie was her cousin.

It made perfect sense, the two of them being English, but it might have been an easier task to deal with a Scot, and Broc cursed the fact that he didn't know the man better.

Piers was reputed to be a fair man, but he was a bloody Sassenach first, and that hadn't changed simply because he'd wed himself to a Highland lass.

From what he recalled of the dispute Montgomerie had had with the Brodies, Montgomerie was a hard man who gave no quarter. Known as King Henry's lion of justice, he was rumored to have a fearful temper, particularly when defending his territory. It was said he'd gone with sword in hand to claim Meghan Brodie from her three brothers and that none of them had dared move to stop him, so fearsome was his wrath at finding Meghan gone from his home. He had stolen her, taken her maidenhead and claimed her for his bride. Broc knew the Brodies well enough to know that none of them feared any man easily. Three more stalwart brothers he'd never met. But Piers had been ready to do battle for the woman he loved, and in the end they'd let her go.

Piers was a formidable man, but Broc knew Meghan would defend him to Piers. And if Meghan loved Montgomerie, as Colin said she did, Montgomerie must be a good man at heart, Sassenach or no. And Elizabet was Piers' own flesh and blood, after all. He shouldn't have to argue her position.

Montgomerie would surely champion her of his own accord.

Och, but his little harridan was beautiful . . . but that was certainly not why he was intervening on her behalf. It was the right thing to do.

Only a year ago he would have loathed her for her Sassenach blood, and in truth, he might have left her to her fate, but much had happened to soften his anger. He still did not trust the English as far as he could toss them, and he thought King David of Scotia a fool for dealing with Henry, for the English would stop at nothing to bring Scotia to its knees. But neither could Broc any longer justify his once blind hatred of the English. He was wary of men like Montgomerie, to be sure, but he could no longer despise them simply for their birth.

And anyway, some good had come of Piers' settlement here. A tentative peace had come to their clans. No longer were ancient feuds, such as that between the MacKinnons and the MacLeans, nursed. No longer did Montgomerie and Brodie war upon one another. Marriage had brought unity to their peoples. Together, the MacLeans, MacKinnons, Brodies and Montgomerie had stood against Page's bastard father.

Broc made his way swiftly through the woodland, telling himself that she would be safe until his return. Though the night was almost too dark to travel, he didn't need much light to make his way. He knew these border woods well.

He heard the voices before he saw them as he broke into the clearing near Montgomerie's manor. He retreated into the woods to assess the scene before continuing.

In the courtyard, two men on horseback with reins to riderless horses in their hands sat their mounts before Montgomerie. Another man stood talking to Piers, and beside them, stretched out upon the ground, lay two bodies. Huddled together on the steps with the newlyweds, Colin and Seana, Broc spied Meghan, with her hand covering her mouth.

Montgomerie held in his hand a parchment, reading from it, and a quiver of dread went down Broc's spine as he awaited his reaction.

Two men were dead, he realized.

He had very likely killed one of them, but not two.

John had been alive when he'd fled with Elizabet. He was certain of it. He hadn't even used his blade upon the man, only the butt of his dagger. There was no way he could have killed him.

No possible way.

His thoughts muddied.

His first consideration was for Elizabet; he had promised her that her brother was alive and well, that he would suffer no more than a headache. How could he return and tell her that he had been mistaken? That he had killed her brother, in truth?

Or had he?

Christ.

If someone had meant Elizabet harm, then so too could he have intended the same for John. Broc must have given the bowman a perfect opportunity.

Remaining at the forest's edge, he moved closer to the party, trying to listen to their discourse, keeping to the trees. But he couldn't get near enough to hear what they were saying, and he grew frustrated.

Who were they blaming?

But he knew.

This did not bode well for him. They would band together, he realized. Who would they blame besides Broc?

Were they all in league together?

A million questions hammered at his brain.

Montgomerie finished the parchment and rolled it very deliberately, fury evident in his gesture. One hand fell to his side, and he clenched it, forming an angry fist.

Broc moved closer, his heart hammering within his chest.

Montgomerie spoke sharply to the men mounted before him, and at once one of them rattled off an explanation that Broc could scarce hear—bits and pieces only.

"Came from nowhere," he heard. And then, "Took us unawares ... stole Elizabet ... killed John and Edmund."

Broc's gaze fell once more to the bodies lying upon the ground.

Bloody liars!

He moved nearer, as close as he dared without risking discovery.

"Fetch my horse!" Montgomerie shouted in command, his tone fraught with anger. "Gather men at once! Meet me before the stables!"

He spun toward the manor as his men scattered to heed his command, leaving Elizabet's traveling companions to await his return. When he was gone, the three of them spoke in low tones to one another, though at this distance, it was impossible to hear what they were saying.

"I'll go and gather my own men and search the north woods," Colin announced and then turned to kiss his bride upon the cheek. He lingered, as though speaking softly at her ear, and then Meghan reached out to embrace her new sister in marriage. The two of them held each other as Colin turned and left them upon the stairs.

What the hell was he going to do about Elizabet?

Broc didn't feel confident enough about going to Piers anymore. He scarce knew Piers, and neither did Piers know him. Why should Piers take his side when it was Broc's word against three of his own compatriots? And one of them was Elizabet's own kinsman.

And what of the bowman? Where was he?

Broc looked closer, trying to make out their faces, but he could barely see more than their silhouettes against the torches lit behind them. He had recognized Piers more than aught else by his stature. He was one of the few men who stood nearly as tall as Broc.

Should he come forward to Colin?

If he did, he would be forced to hand Elizabet over to Piers. He was certain Colin would bid him do so. And in doing that, he would place her once more in danger. Nor, in truth, could he expect Colin to keep his confidence in such a serious matter. He would risk a blood feud between Piers and Meghan's brothers. He couldn't allow that.

And he couldn't take Elizabet to Iain either. The last thing he wished to do was force his own laird to take a stand against Montgomerie. This wasn't Iain's problem.

Christ and bedamned.

What options did he have?

None, it seemed, save to return to Elizabet and tell her what had happened.

Except that her brother was dead now, and Broc couldn't prove it wasn't by his hand.

The riders were beginning to disperse now, and he didn't wish to lead them to Elizabet, so he thought it best to go.

Cursing himself for the mess he had managed to create, he turned and fled into the woods. Not daring to look back, he raced through the forest, weaving blindly through the trees in the darkness, relying on instinct to guide him.

Only one thing did he know for certain. No

longer at stake was her life alone. Regardless of whether or not he chose to let her go, the blame for her brother's death would fall to Broc, and the peace that had fallen over the MacKinnon, Brodie, and Montgomerie clans would be no more.

Without doubt, his laird would stand behind him, as would Colin. Piers might love his wife, but Elizabet and her brother John were his own flesh and blood, and he would surely champion them. Unless Broc could bring John's murderer to light, his own clan would surely be forced to take up arms against Montgomerie—and mayhap Colin against his sister's husband.

Broc couldn't bear to have the blood of his kinsmen on his hands, but neither could he in good conscience simply hand over Elizabet to her murderer.

Not to mention the fact that Elizabet would just as likely name him as her brother's murderer along with her Sassenach companions, and where would that leave him?

When he reached the hovel, he was drenched in his own sweat and reluctant to go in. He fell upon his knees to catch his breath.

What the bloody hell was he supposed to say when he faced her? Her trust in him was tentative at best. No matter how he looked at the situation, he was damned either way.

Och, but what a pretty kettle of fish he had boiled himself within.

It almost made a man wish he'd never gotten out of bed.

Chapter 8

It had occurred to Elizabet only after he'd gone that she didn't even know his name.

Her mother would have surely scolded her for trusting her life into this man's hands, but Elizabet somehow sensed he meant her no harm. She didn't know how she knew it. She simply did.

Growing impatient for his return now, she paced the small hovel, trying not to note the stale, dank odor of the room. She grimaced with disgust as she walked through a sticky web and tried to shrug free of it.

How could anyone live like this?

His *friend's* house, was it?

It wasn't her experience that men and women could be friends. She couldn't help but wonder just how close they had been, her Scotsman and this woman who had wed his best friend.

Had they been lovers?

Likely so!

She clasped her hands at her back and continued to pace, considering the sparseness of the room.

What sort of woman lived in a place such as this?

Elizabet had never really owned anything herself, but she had never gone without the most basic of necessities. She had been surrounded by luxuries. Her mother's lovers had all been generous, at least.

She reached down to clasp the crucifix in her hand, taking comfort in it.

The woman who had lived here probably had missing teeth, else her Good Samaritan Scotsman would have claimed her as more than his beloved friend. He had probably used her until someone else had been willing to take her off his hands.

Wind gusted into the room through cracks in the wall and ceiling. The candle on the table sputtered, threatening to go out. Elizabet hugged herself for warmth. She searched the room for a blanket and, finding one, seized it and threw it about her shoulders. It was threadbare and reeked of fermented drink, the odor permeating every fiber of the material. Sweet Jesu, the woman had been a bloody drunkard, as well!

Then again—her gaze took in the tiny room once more—if she had been forced to live in a place like this, she might have taken to drink, too.

It shouldn't surprise her. These Scots were rumored to be partial to their ale. They were all barbarians, every one of them, women and children as well. But they all shared one thing more valuable than any material possession Elizabet might have had.

Their freedom.

Elizabet had heard much about the way they lived. Even the women seemed to enjoy a certain mastery over their lives. They wed where they pleased and not at all if 'twas their wish. And their children ran about dirty and free. The men loved their brides and wed not for duty but for life. They had no need to keep mistresses on the side. Their mistresses were their wives.

As much as Elizabet loved her mother, her sympathies had oft lain with the wives of the men who had visited her. And she had hoped never to marry if it meant that her husband would lavish his affections upon women like her mother and leave her to rot at home, like some forgotten trophy set upon a shelf.

She'd rather be alone.

Only not here.

A grimace turned her lips as the shadows deepened.

It was no wonder that when she heard a sound outside, she rushed to the door, throwing it open. It had grown black, the sky dark as pitch. The sounds of small animals scurrying through the underbrush made her jump in alarm. It had hardly been so frightening to hear those sounds when she'd traveled with her brother and her father's men, but now she saw murderers in every bush.

Unnerved by the near moonless night, she pulled the door shut, shuddering, though not entirely from the cold. Anticipation of Broc's return kept her on her feet. Concern for her brother made her pace the small room.

What made her heart beat so swiftly?

Her fingers went to her lips, remembering . . .

He'd kissed her in anger, but he hadn't hurt her. Still, he'd taken liberties she had never offered any man. And now she couldn't forget the warmth of his mouth upon her lips. Every time she recalled, her heart jolted violently within her breast.

Why couldn't she stop thinking about him? And his mouth in particular? With all that had transpired that afternoon—the bowman, her brother—the one instant that kept playing over and over in her head was the moment he had taken her into his arms.

What was wrong with her?

She tried to focus on the important matters.

How long had he been gone now? It seemed like an eternity.

What would Piers say?

They must be very near Montgomerie's fief, as her guardian angel seemed to know Piers well. Then again, an Englishman with holdings in Scotia would most likely be prattled about for leagues. She knew these Scots couldn't like Montgomerie's presence here. Nor would they relish that he'd been given King David's approval. Nor that he was a favored emissary of King Henry.

Had he merely been trying to teach her a lesson, or was it something more?

Heat crept into her face as she remembered his arousal.

She needn't fool herself into believing it was something more. All men awoke with an arousal—or so her mother had claimed.

God's truth, she wished he would hurry.

The night seemed to be getting colder by the instant, and, as the candle grew shorter, the shadows grew longer. Wrapping the blanket more firmly about her shoulders, she sat again at the little table to wait, anxious to learn something of her brother.

Mayhap she should set out by herself to find Piers? She felt entirely too helpless waiting here in this place. She was wholly unaccustomed to taking such a passive approach to her affairs.

There had never been anyone to champion her, not ever, not even as a child. Her mother had been far too busy with her own life, and if Elizabet had wanted something, she'd had to pursue it herself.

This wait was driving her mad!

Where the devil was he?

Growing too impatient to remain seated, she sprang from the chair and went to the door once more, throwing it open with a vengeance. The last thing she expected to find was her dubious savior standing there, leaning with one hand on the doorframe, staring down at his feet, as though he had nary a concern in the world.

She shrieked in alarm.

He bellowed in surprise.

"What are you doing here?" she exclaimed.

He stood and turned to face her, narrowing his eyes at her. "Picking flowers," he answered sardonically.

He was alone. Something had not gone well by the look on his face. "How long have you been standing there?" she demanded to know.

"Not verra long."

She pushed the door open wider, allowing him entrance, and he walked past her without looking into her eyes.

Elizabet waited for him to explain.

Sweet Mary, had Piers repudiated her? Panic

assailed her. What would she do if he turned her away?

"He wasn't there."

Her heart fluttered. "Piers?"

"Aye." He turned to face her at last, and Elizabet felt her knees go weak at his glance. Never in her life had she met eyes so vivid a blue. "He's gone to Edinburgh and willna be back for a few days."

Averting her gaze, Elizabet went to the table and sat, considering his news. How could she stay here alone with this man for all that time? Yet how could she risk leaving?

When she met his gaze again, he was watching her, his blue eyes assessing.

"You cannot expect me to wait here until he returns," she declared suddenly. "My brother will worry. Neither do I wish to leave him alone." Though John was the elder, Elizabet felt responsible for him. She wasn't about to degrade him by saying so, but she would worry nevertheless.

She just couldn't stay here!

He met her declaration with absolute silence.

Broc had decided his best course was to tell her the truth, because he didn't know how to lie. But faced with her now, he didn't know how to tell her that her brother was in fact dead. He tried to speak the words, but they wouldn't come.

"He must know what has happened here. I

must tell him," she insisted, and his guilt escalated. He hadn't killed the man, but he knew she would believe that he had. And if she thought he'd murdered her brother, there was no way she would willingly remain with him. Her life was in danger, he reasoned. He couldn't tell her the truth.

For an instant, he feared he'd spoken his thoughts aloud.

She sprang from the chair. "You told me my brother was unharmed!"

He shook his head. "He's fine, lass. But he was surrounded." That much was true. "I simply could not speak with him."

She stared at him hopefully. "But you swear he is unharmed?"

Broc swallowed the truth, unwilling to tell her just yet. "Aye, he's fine." In truth the man was feeling no pain.

She sat again, her hand going to her breast as though in relief. Broc tried not to notice the way her fingers lit so gently upon the curve of her bosom, taunting him with their very right to be there.

When was the last time he had held a woman's soft breast? When was the last time he had missed it?

Scarce a handful of times had he allowed himself the pleasure—and even then not without guilt. He'd made a vow to himself years ago to devote his life to his clan, to forswear his own gratification. On a few occasions he had forgotten himself in the throes of drink—he was no saint—but never had he with a clear mind been tempted by any wench. He hadn't cared to add to his burdens. His loyalty and his life belonged to the MacKinnons and Iain's family, Page and little Malcom. They were his primary concern. He owed Iain everything. There was nothing left of him to give to anyone else.

Broc took the chair across from her, watching her expressions as she deliberated.

She made him crave things he hadn't ever dared contemplate.

"What now?"

It was a damned good question.

She looked so forlorn, so vulnerable, and he vowed to protect her at all costs. He hadn't felt so moved by a pair of sultry green eyes since he'd been a child. He didn't know why he felt responsible for her, but from the instant he'd spied Elizabet alone in the forest, he had felt drawn to her somehow.

She needed him, and he refused to abandon her.

"Elizabet . . ." He leaned forward. "I know ye dinna like the idea of staying in this place, but I gi' ye my word ye will be safe as long as ye remain."

Her brows slanted. "I don't know . . ."

"If ye wish it, I will even stay with ye, but ye must trust me!" he pleaded with her.

She stared at the table, obviously torn.

"If I had meant ye harm," he reasoned with her, "would I have let ye remain here alone whilst I went to speak with Montgomerie?"

She seemed to think about it a moment and then shook her head.

"Nay," he asserted. "I wouldna have. And I am tellin' ye I saw a bowman, and he was dressed in the same livery as the rest of your companions."

She shook her head, denying his testimony, though he sensed deep down she must believe him. She would never have waited here for him otherwise. "He might simply have been defending me," she reasoned.

"Och! Think about it, lass. Would he have tried to kill me simply for speaking to ye? Was there a need to defend ye when we were only bantering?"

Again she shook her head. "I cannot fathom why he should wish me dead."

It seemed to Broc that she knew who the bowman might be.

"I was not the object of his attention," Broc persisted, trying to make her believe.

Her brows knit. "He was kind to me and to my brother the entire journey."

"Aye, well . . . 'tis said ye win more flies with honey."

Her shoulders slumped. She peered up at him, her eyes full of indecision. "How long before Piers returns?"

Broc needed time, time to expose the bowman. "Three, mayhap four days," he told her, shrugging.

"Sweet Jesu! That long?"

Every lie seemed to come easier. " 'Tis what his wife said."

She blinked her eyes in surprise, then cocked her head at that revelation. "Piers has a wife?"

"Meghan," he told her. "He wed her little more than two months past."

She peered down at the table and then up again.

He placed his heart in his eyes; he willed her to see it. "I willna let ye down, Elizabet. Ye have my word."

"Very well," she conceded at last, "I'll stay. Though with one condition. You must seek out my brother and tell him where I am. Bring him to me if you can."

Broc swallowed his guilt but nodded agreement. "I'll do it first thing on the morrow."

Chapter 9

He gave her the blanket and the pallet and slept on the floor across the room.

Elizabet had never been more aware of someone's presence. She could hear every breath he took, knew every time he tossed in his sleep.

Or was he asleep?

They had doused the lights over an hour ago, but she still could not close her eyes. When she did, she saw not her brother lying on the forest floor or the image of a bowman in the woods but this Scotsman standing over her, handing her the blankets to wrap herself in. She had lain upon the pallet, shivering, until he'd come to her, because she hadn't wished to take the lone blanket when she'd already claimed the pallet and he was left with the floor.

Since his return, he hadn't been the least familiar with her, keeping to himself, in fact, as though she were cursed with some terrible disease. She might have thought he was repulsed by her, except that when he looked at her, she didn't see revulsion at all.

She saw that same look he'd given her earlier . . . when he'd kissed her.

She had been certain he would expect payment for his troubles. And she had hesitated to remain alone with him for fear of it, yet since his return, he had treated her with nothing but respect and kindness.

She did believe him. He didn't strike her as a man who would lie. Nor could she perceive one single reason he would concoct such a story simply to have her alone when in truth he could have had his way with her when first he encountered her in the woods. Looking back on it, he might have killed her easily in those first moments before her brother and her father's men had come after them.

Aye, she *did* believe him.

Or did she simply wish to?

What she really wished was that he weren't asleep.

How could he sleep so peacefully when she was wide awake?

Above her, slivers of moonlight stabbed through the roof like fine-edged knives. Tiny flying insects dove into the light and out again. Elizabet watched them with a sense of growing agitation.

She still didn't know his name.

She wasn't at all certain why she hadn't simply asked, except that somehow it seemed too personal. They were hardly friends.

He'd promised to seek out her brother first thing in the morn. Likely he was anticipating a quick end to this ordeal. After all, this wasn't his problem. It was hers.

Still and all, how could he leave her alone tonight with her thoughts in a place such as this? He might be sleeping in the same room, but his presence alone wasn't enough to save her from brooding.

"Are you sleeping?" she whispered before she could stop herself.

There was no answer save a snort.

She said it louder. "Hey . . . are you sleeping?"

Still no answer.

"Well, of course you are!" she muttered to herself, and couldn't explain the sudden sense of disappointment she felt at discovering it was so.

"Jesu!"

Why should she care if her presence wasn't enough to keep him awake. Why did she feel so vexed that he was sleeping so contentedly in his little corner of the room?

In truth, she might owe him a debt for saving her life and for helping her, but that didn't

change the fact that he was a rude, discourteous
Scot!

She kicked the too short blanket down over
her feet. She just couldn't sleep, and it was colder
than she'd ever remembered it being in her life.
And she couldn't fathom how he could sleep so
obliviously! He must be made of stone! Her fingers and toes had long since gone numb. And
her teeth were chattering. She pulled the covers
up and curled her legs more tightly beneath her,
trying to ward off the chill.

"You never even troubled yourself to tell me
your name!" she hissed into the darkness.

"Because ye never bothered to ask," he replied
at once.

Her heart jolted at the sound of his voice.

What the devil was she supposed to say to him
now? "I . . . uh . . . thought you were asleep."

Broc smiled to himself. That much was obvious.

"So it seems."

God's teeth, how the hell could he sleep when
he knew she was lying so near. Without doubt,
she was the most lovely woman he had ever set
eyes on in his life, Sassenach or no, and no matter that he tried not to see her through male eyes,
he could not suppress the images that had come
to haunt his waking dreams.

God's truth, he hadn't wished her to know he
was awake, because it was easier to deny his de-

sire if he didn't have to speak to her and hear
her voice, if he didn't have to look at her face by
candlelight and wonder how many other men
had gazed into those lovely green eyes.

He was quickly becoming obsessed with
thoughts about her. "They call me Broc Ceannfhionn."

"Broc . . . Ceannfhionn," she repeated, and was
silent a moment, as though considering his
name.

"It means Broc the Blond."

"Ah . . . well, that makes sense. You are fair."

What was he supposed to say to that? Was it
a good thing to be fair? Did she find him as beautiful as he found her? His face burned at the
thought. Well, she likely did not think him beautiful . . . mayhap comely. Men were not beautiful,
but comely would be good, he thought.

"Tell me about yourself, Broc Ceannfhionn."

God's teeth, he was unaccustomed to making
idle chatter, particularly with highborn English
women. And he was even less comfortable talking about himself.

"Well, I dinna have fleas anymore," he told
her, and hoped she appreciated that fact. Thanks
to Page, he no longer walked about scratching
his head like some mangy beast. He'd loved his
Merry fiercely, but fleas were certainly one thing
he didn't miss about her.

He thought he heard her giggle, but it was so

soft a sound he couldn't be certain. He wouldn't blame her for laughing. What an idiot he must sound like. Put him face to face with a woman he wanted to bed, and he suddenly became an imbecile.

"Well . . . I don't have fleas either," she countered, her tone slightly amused, and he understood she was mocking him.

He felt his cheeks grow warmer but grinned despite himself.

Wench.

He wanted to know all about her, everything. Who was her father? Who was her mother? How long was she to remain in Scotia? Was she in love with some fortunate man? Had she come to be wed? Had her father sent her to Piers to be bartered in marriage?

Broc winced at the thought.

He hoped not.

Neither of them spoke for the longest time, and the hut fell silent save for the chattering of her teeth.

He lay there, yearning for the sound of her voice, at least. His body was taut with desire, and for the first time in his life, he burned. No simple longing was this. Nay. The more he tried to deny it, the more he hungered for the salt taste of her flesh, the more he thirsted for the nectar of her body. He was glad for the darkness of the room that hid the evidence of his desire. Had he a blanket, he would have easily erected himself a tent large enough to fit the both of them.

Her teeth continued to chatter.

"Are ye cold, lass?" His voice was thick with lust, he knew, but he hoped she wouldn't notice.

"In all my days I never imagined a summer night could be so wintry!"

He chuckled at her lighthearted complaint. " 'Tis the Highlands for ye."

"I suppose."

Once again silence fell between them.

Broc wondered what else to say to her. He didn't really want her to go to sleep just yet. He wanted to know more. Where did she grow up? And what was her favorite color?

She saved him the effort of finding suitable conversation. "How well do you know Piers?"

"Not verra well at all."

"I see."

She went silent again, and Broc knit his brows, at a loss. Never had his palms sweated so much when Meghan spoke to him, lovely though she was. What was wrong with him?

He was as courtly as a backwoods drunkard!

"So . . . have ye come to wed?" he asked her far more bluntly than he'd intended.

"Me?" He heard her turn toward him upon her pallet, and he tried to imagine what she looked like lying there in the dark. It was far too dark to see. "Oh, nay!" she exclaimed.

He nearly sighed in relief.

"My father merely thought we would fare better with Piers. My brothers and sisters are many. He hadn't enough to provide for us all."

Her disclosure left him feeling envious. He'd always wondered what it would be like to have siblings. In fact, he'd had a baby sister, though she'd been far too young to withstand the attack when the English had raped his village. She'd died in his mother's arms. He scarce remembered her. Erin had been her name. How old would she be now? It gave him a prickle of guilt that he couldn't recall. He'd been seven when he'd come to the MacKinnons. His sister had been mayhap two at the time of her death. And it had been nearly twenty-three years since he'd come to Chreagach Mhor.

He pushed the memories away and resolved not to let Elizabet down.

Except that he already had.

Her brother was dead.

"We *will* discover who the bowman is, lass. Dinna fear. I willna allow him to harm ye."

This time her silence was fraught with worry. He could hear it in her voice when she spoke again. "I hope my brother will be safe, as well."

The lie weighed heavily upon him. "I'm certain he will be." God help him for not telling her the truth. It would come later to haunt him, he knew, but it couldn't be helped.

For the longest time neither of them spoke. Night sounds filled his ears. The scent of her drifted to his nose—sweet, warm flesh.

"You must be cold," she said after a time.

His heart beat faster, anticipating the sound of her voice. "A bit."

"Would you . . . like the blanket?" she surprised him by asking. "I've the pallet, after all. 'Tis only fair you should have the blanket."

Broc lay speechless at her gesture.

Not since his mother died had anyone cared whether he'd eaten, whether he was cold, or whether he had a soft place to lay his head at night. Since he'd been a wee child, he'd fended for himself. That this Englishwoman would concern herself over his comfort—and more, that she would offer to ease his misery at her own expense—moved him more than he liked to admit.

His throat grew thicker yet. "Nay," he croaked, refusing her offer outright.

His intentions weren't entirely noble when he suggested, "But we could share it?"

He winced, waiting for her to become incensed by the proposition, but she surprised him by replying, "It *is* cold . . ." Her teeth chattered softly.

Broc's heart jolted at the veiled agreement.

There was the smallest note of appeal in her voice.

Mayhap, for her sake, he should have refused

once more, but she promised to warm him in a way he hadn't ever been warmed before. He could not deny himself the sweet pleasure of her warm body at his side.

Chapter 10

Elizabet heard him rise.

She squeezed her eyes shut and listened to his footsteps as he approached. He stopped abruptly at her side, peering down. Her heart beat wildly against her breasts, and her breath was labored as she waited for him to speak.

In truth, she'd hoped he would lie down with her, comfort her with his presence, but she hadn't really expected him to acquiesce. Not since his return from Montgomerie's had he made the slightest advance toward her, and he'd planted himself to sleep as far from her as he possibly could without putting himself out the door.

His actions perplexed her.

One minute he was telling her she was beautiful, kissing her passionately, the next he seemed loath even to look at her. And now he was standing before her in the darkness, waiting.

"Are ye certain, lass?" he asked her, his voice deep and rich.

Jesu, but she wasn't certain of anything at all.

Only now that he was standing before her, she couldn't turn him away. Some little voice deep inside her sounded an alarm, but she strangled it, refusing its counsel.

She swallowed and said, "Aye."

She lifted the blanket at once to allow him access, and her throat became suddenly too thick to speak. Her heart pounding fiercely as he settled beside her, she remained silent. He took the covers from her, drawing them high about the both of them, and shock pummeled her at the reality of his body beside her. She had never lain with any man, not even to ease the chill.

He seemed so big, so solid, lying there. His heat permeated her entire body at once, and the chill of the night was forgotten as she lay quaking beside him.

Without a word, he drew her close, enfolding her in his arms. "You're trembling," he said.

Elizabet nodded in response. "C-Cold," she lied.

He nestled himself more snugly against her, lifting a hand to her nape in an attempt to weave his fingers into her hair. The tightness of her plait prevented it.

"Och, lass, how can ye sleep wi' your hair bound so tight?"

"I-I'm a-accustomed to it," Elizabet stuttered.

"Ye would sleep more soundly, I'd wager, with your hair set free."

He didn't ask permission to unbind her plait, but his fingers skimmed the length of her hair and began to work the ribbons loose.

Elizabet couldn't find her voice to protest as his fingers worked deftly, removing her bindings. When the ribbons were free at last, his fingers began to undo her plait.

Elizabet closed her eyes, trying to still the erratic beating of her heart. She could feel his heart pounding against her cheek, fierce as her own.

"So soft," he whispered against her forehead, and the warmth of his lips increased her shivers. The memory of his kiss suffused her with heat.

God help her, she wanted him to kiss her again. She wanted it more than anything she had ever desired.

Elizabet buried her face against his chest, her cheeks burning. His fingers combed through her hair, smoothing through the curls. Her entire body came alive. Every inch of her flesh tingled with awareness.

Kiss me, she silently begged him.

"Do ye never wear it loose?" he whispered.

"Nay," she croaked, forcing the reply. Her mouth became parched, and she swallowed.

"Why not?" he asked her. " 'Tis lovely, lovely hair ye have."

No one had ever touched her so gently. No man had ever embraced her so intimately. The soft sound of his voice disarmed her. The warmth of his body made her flesh burn, and the gentleness of his touch sent prickles of pleasure down her spine.

Kiss me, she silently begged him.

It was all Broc could do not to seduce her where she lay.

He wanted to—God, he wanted to. She was pressed so tightly against his body, though suggestively or defensively he couldn't tell. Only one thing was certain; she was trembling.

Was she afeared?

Was she merely cold?

His body didn't seem to care which. His response was immediate and hard.

He wanted to kiss her, craved her mouth more than anything. From the instant he'd kissed her this afternoon, the taste of her had clung to his senses. The scent of her remained on his clothes, taunting him.

He should have asked, mayhap, but he couldn't bear for her to refuse him. Like a drunkard seeking his ale, he bent to drink of her mouth, fevered for the taste of her. His fingers closed about her nape, and he lowered his mouth to her lips, praying she would welcome him.

The instant his mouth lit upon hers, he was filled with incredible bliss. She tasted of heaven itself. His hands combed her silken hair. His body hardened fully, throbbed with desire. When had he ever needed a woman so desperately? When had he more feverishly craved two legs wrapped about his waist? God himself couldn't have lifted him from her in that instant, so intoxicated was he by the taste of her.

Elizabet moaned softly, and he answered her cries with deeper groans of pleasure.

Surely, she had died and gone to heaven. The shock of his kiss set her senses reeling. He kissed her gently, caressing her mouth with his moist, hot lips, and she moaned in pleasure and in protest. Some part of her warned her to object . . . now . . . before she gave too much—before he took it too far.

But his kiss was too insistent, and her heart was pounding too fiercely.

His arms wrapped more firmly about her, holding her for the onslaught of his mouth. His legs entwined with hers, pressing his hardness against her, and she lifted her body instinctively, seeking his arousal.

She was playing a dangerous game, she knew, but she could scarce think to stop it. If he should choose to force himself on her, there was no one about to hear her scream.

Her body betrayed her.

Was she no different from her mother?

Nay, she was not. She wanted him never to stop. No longer was she cold, but feverishly hot. His hands began to caress her body, lavishing such incredible tenderness upon her flesh that she could only moan in ecstacy.

And then, when she thought her heart could beat no faster, his scalding tongue swept out to caress her lips, moistening them with his own ambrosia.

"Open for me," he begged her.

Elizabet swallowed and did as he bade her, allowing him entrance. His tongue delved within the instant she parted her lips.

"Your taste is sweet," he whispered into her mouth, and groaned. "So sweet . . ."

Elizabet clung to him, undulating softly beneath him, her senses clouded in a fever of lust.

He pressed himself against her, answering her every gentle thrust with one of his own. His hands swept down over her hip, down her thigh, clutched at her hem, lifted her dress. Elizabet's heart flipped inside her breast.

"Open for me," he whispered once more, pressing gently against the inside of her thigh, and Elizabet listened dumbly, unable to resist.

He lifted a hand to her most private place, thumbing the delicate bead of her womanhood. His finger slid over her moistness with tender deftness, as though he understood precisely how to tease her. And all the while he kissed her senseless, sharing her breath, giving it back. It was the most incredible moment of her entire life.

And then suddenly he slipped a finger inside her body and froze. She felt his heart thunder against her breast, but the haze of pleasure had yet to clear enough for her to comprehend what he had done—what he was doing—what she had allowed.

God help her, it wasn't until that instant that she found the will to resist.

In panic, she pounded his shoulder with a fist. He rolled off her, and she tore herself out of his arms, scrambling away. "Get away from me!" she demanded.

He didn't answer, didn't stir, merely lay there in stony silence, staring up at her in the darkness.

Elizabet glared at him accusingly, though she knew he could not spy her face. God's truth, she wasn't certain who she was more angry with, Broc or herself. He was a man, after all, and she should have expected no less from him, but she should have known better than to invite him under her covers.

What was wrong with her? She was, in truth, no better than her mother! What had she done?

"You're no different from the rest!" she spat at him in anger and shame.

When he still made no advance toward her,

she backed herself into a corner and sat, tears clouding her eyes. He had the blanket and the pallet now, but she didn't care. It served her right for being such a silly fool. How close she had come! How easily she would have given him her most precious possession! She swallowed convulsively, shame washing over her.

He said nothing more, nor did he move. And he must have fallen asleep shortly thereafter, because she heard his smooth, even breath from where she sat.

But sleep eluded her until deep into the night.

He listened to her weep and cursed himself for being so base.

Somehow, she managed to sleep, despite the cold, despite her sorrow, and Broc returned the blanket to her, tucking it gently about her slender body. She slept on, oblivious to his ministrations. And in spite of his guilt, he managed to fall asleep after.

In the morning, he left her sleeping and hurried to Chreagach Mhor. Iain would wonder where he'd been.

He was torn.

Some part of him felt obliged to tell Iain everything. His laird had always stood behind him. But thereabouts lay the problem. How could he live with himself if he involved Iain in this deception? He had no idea how to resolve this. Nor did he truly wish Elizabet to hear news of her brother until he was ready for her to know it. He felt responsible.

What was he to do?

The village below Chreagach Mhor's soaring keep was just now awaking. He could hear his little cousin's giggles somewhere in the distance and a dog barking, as well. The familiar sounds left him wistful, because it wasn't Merry Constance was harassing this morn.

"Where the hell ha'e ye been?" his cousin Cameron asked, rushing up to greet him. Cameron skipped backwards, facing Broc, and judging by the eager look upon his face, was excited by something he was about to share.

"I slept at Colin's," Broc replied, and his face warmed with the untruth. He wasn't a very good liar, but he didn't seem to have a choice in the matter. He still hadn't decided whether or not he was going to tell Iain. But Cameron was not the sort to keep confidences, and he was the last person Broc would confide in, cousin or no.

"At Colin's!" Surprise was apparent in Cameron's tone. "Och, man! On his wedding night, Broc?" He stopped for an instant, staring at Broc as though he thought him mad.

Broc kept walking, ignoring him. "Christ and bedamned!" he exploded. "I didna say I slept in their bed, Cameron!"

His rebuke didn't begin to dampen Cameron's

good humor. He caught up to Broc once more and thrust his callow grin into Broc's face. "And whose bed di' ye sleep in, then?" He wiggled his brows. "Tell me!"

Broc arched a brow at his cousin. "That," he told him, "would be none of your concern."

"Damn ye, Broc! Dinna speak to me as though I were a wee bairn! I'm old enough to bed my own woman."

"So ye are," Broc relented.

"Anyway," Cameron continued, " 'tis about damned time ye removed your saint's cap. I ha'e seen the way ye look at Page FitzSimon!"

Broc halted abruptly, leveling his young cousin a warning look. The very thought of bedding Page made Broc's stomach roil. "Boy, dinna ever speak like that again about your laird's wife! I would cut out your tongue myself if Iain doesna beat me to it!"

Cameron's smile wilted. "Damn," he said. "I was merely jesting wi' ye, ye sour-tempered oaf!"

"Aye, well, dinna jest about that ever again!" Broc advised him and started walking once more toward the storage house.

Cameron threw up his hands and followed.

Broc intended only to gather his supplies and go. Elizabet would likely be waking soon, and he didn't wish to frighten her by his absence.

Then again she might wish never to see him after last night.

"Good Christ, what bug crawled up your arse? I ha'e never seen ye so surly."

Broc gave his cousin a beleaguered glance. "If my temper is sour, 'tis because my whereabouts are my own concern, Cameron, not yours. Dinna ye ever forget that."

"Och, mon! Forget it! I dinna ken what's gotten into ye this morn, but I wager ye're as cantankerous as a drunk without his whiskey!"

"I didn't sleep well last night," Broc explained. And it was true. His conscience had bedeviled him.

Cameron opened his mouth to speak again, but after taking one look at Broc's expression, he obviously thought better of it. He closed it again.

God's teeth, Broc had hoped to gather his supplies and be gone before anyone noticed him. It seemed that was not going to be the case this morn. Constance spotted him suddenly and came barreling toward him, calling out his name.

For her, he managed a bright smile. His youngest cousin was a joyful child who never went five minutes without laughter spilling from her lips.

"Broc! Broc!" she screamed, and threw her arms open wide.

Broc stooped to catch her. "Brat!" he exclaimed as she hurled herself into his arms. She giggled, and he tousled her hair, lifting her up.

"Ha'e ye heard the news?" Cameron asked him then.

"What news?"

"Two Englishmen were slain in the woods near Chreagach Mhor."

Broc's stomach turned, but he pretended an aloofness he didn't feel. "Aye, well, serves the bastards right for being where they dinna belong!"

Constance strangled his neck and then suddenly let him go. "Down!" she demanded.

"One of them was Montgomerie's kin," Cameron added darkly. "Montgomerie is furious."

Broc feigned a smile for Constance's sake. "I want down!" she shrieked, and he set her down at once, patting her on the head. She ran away to play. "Be good, brat," he called after her.

"We're going to have to lock her up someday, I think," Broc commented.

Cameron was fixed to his tale. "Apparently a woman has gone missing, as well," he persisted. "Montgomerie and Meghan's brothers have gotten together a search party for her. I think Piers will not rest until he sees the man brought to justice."

Broc started to walk, pretending only a casual interest. "Do they know who killed them?"

"Nay. No one knows," his cousin revealed. "But they claim it was a giant!"

Broc rolled his eyes.

"Aye! They say he had arms as big as his thighs and a neck as big as the thickest tree!"

Broc glanced down at his arms and then back at his cousin, screwing up his face. He was a big man, but och!

He cast his cousin a disbelieving glance. "And does he blow smoke from his nostrils and are his teeth as long and sharp as daggers?"

" 'Tis what they are claiming," Cameron assured him.

Broc shook his head. "Idiot Sassenachs. 'Tis because their vanity cannot handle the simple fact that their puny arses are no match for a Scotsman!"

Cameron chortled. " 'Tis the bloody truth!" he agreed. "At any rate, they've every clan within ten leagues up in arms over it all."

Broc gritted his teeth. "And what has Iain to say over it all?"

"He will back Montgomerie, he says. He willna allow any man to endanger the alliances formed these past few months. 'Tis too precious, he says."

It *was* too precious. It had taken Iain's entire lifetime to achieve it. Broc couldn't ask him to risk it. It wouldn't be right. "I canna say I blame him," he said, and sighed.

"Nor I," Cameron agreed soberly, sounding more man in that instant than Broc had ever witnessed. "Sassenach or no, Montgomerie is here to stay, it seems, and 'twould behoove us to back him."

Broc stopped and turned to his cousin, taking his measure. The lad was maturing, Broc was pleased to see. He reached out, smacking him on the shoulder. "That he is, Cam. That he is."

Cameron smiled at Broc's silent praise, and the two of them shared a moment of kinship.

"I think Iain wishes to speak to ye," Cameron told him after.

It was the last thing Broc wished to hear.

He couldn't face him.

Iain would surely know him for a liar.

"Tell him I will meet with him anon."

Cameron blinked, surprised by his response, Broc knew. He had never declined a summons from Iain before. He started again toward the storage and didn't stop, refusing to look into Cameron's eyes. He didn't wish to give explanations just now and didn't want questions asked. He didn't want to lie any more than he had to.

Cameron was nonplussed. He didn't follow. "Where are you going?"

Broc didn't answer.

He picked up his pace, leaving Cameron to stare after him, silent in his bewilderment.

Iain MacKinnon stood with arms akimbo.

His wife rose from the table to join him.

He and Page had remained at table long after the breaking of their fast, discussing the news that had been delivered at first rising. And now he couldn't believe what Cameron was telling him. He narrowed his eyes at the youth, disbelieving his claim. "You say he came and left again?"

Cameron nodded, his look apologetic.

"And you told him I wished to speak with him?"

"Aye, sir, I did."

Iain knew the boy still felt bad about his dealings with Page's lunatic father. And well he should. He'd nearly gotten his own sister, little Constance, murdered by the madman and had endangered the life of his laird's wife. On top of that he was responsible for the death of poor Merry, Broc's dog. God's truth, there had been not a dry eye in the village at the sight of Broc burying his beloved companion. If Cameron knew what was good for him, he would tread warily for some time to come.

"He said he would speak to you anon," the youth added, screwing up his face in obvious distress. Iain was certain Cameron didn't wish to tell him that his cousin had declined the summons. It was obvious by his expression. One thing Iain knew of a certain was that Cameron looked up to Broc. Far more than a cousin, Broc was like a father to the lad.

Iain had no idea what to say. Broc had never rebuffed him. No matter what his own business, Broc had always set his affairs aside for the time it took to meet with Iain, particularly since Iain never summoned him unless the matter was urgent. He didn't make it a habit to interrupt his clansmen's lives frivolously.

Page came and set a hand upon his shoulder. "Tis unlike him, Iain."

"Aye." In truth, Iain couldn't imagine what circumstances would have Broc so preoccupied that he would deny Iain a few moments of his time. He frowned at Cameron, and the boy took a step back in self-preservation. It wasn't Cameron's fault that Broc had rebuffed him, but Iain didn't bother to set him at ease. Mayhap he would think twice next time he considered interfering in his laird's affairs.

Page added, "I'm told he didn't come home last night."

"Aye, my lady," Cameron interjected, giving his laird's wife proper deference. He peered up at Iain, and Iain smiled slightly in approval. "Because he stayed at Colin's."

"Jesu!" Page exclaimed.

"On his wedding night?" both Iain and Page asked at once.

Cameron shrugged. "I'm only tellin' ye what he told me, sir."

Iain shook his head in wonder. "Christ, I've

never known Broc to lie," he said at once. "If he said he stayed at Colin's, then he stayed at Colin's, though I'd like to have been there to witness that!"

Page's brows drew together. "Whatever do you mean?"

Cameron snickered, and Iain explained, "Everyone knows Colin's bride had a sweet spot for Broc. Considering that fact, I suppose Colin may have had a less traditional wedding night in mind."

Page smacked her husband on the arm.

Iain winked at her. "Mere suggestion, my dear, mere suggestion."

Page arched a censuring brow. "Men!" she declared. "Ye are all depraved!"

Iain merely laughed at that.

He loved the wench, temper and all.

Cameron laughed as well, though a little nervously. "Well, Colin always was a raunchy one," he proposed, "but Broc said it wasna like that at all."

Iain put his arm about his beautiful wife and drew her into his embrace. He loved her more every moment he spent with her. "Depraved I may verra well be, my love," he assured her, "but you are the only woman I care to have in my bed."

Cameron's face reddened at their banter.

Page's smile ruined her rebuke. "If you know

what's good for you, you'd better say so, husband!"

He hugged her possessively, smiled and, un-
fazed by her threat, turned again to Cameron. "I
have no inkling what to say."

He wasn't angry at all, though he'd wished to
speak with Broc about the murders to see if he'd
heard anything at all. "I suppose whatever he's
doing is of utmost importance. I'll talk to him
when he returns. Thanks for the message," he
said, dismissing the boy once and for all.

Cameron turned to go, and Iain turned to his
wife.

Her brows knit, and she seemed to be thinking—he hoped not the same as he. The description given him of the murderer had matched
Broc in part, though he'd dismissed the possibility it might be him as soon as it had entered his
thoughts. As described, the slaying was far too
brutal and far too cold-blooded to have been
committed by a man such as Broc Ceannfhionn.

They'd claimed the man had assaulted the
party without provocation, leaping out upon
their mistress from the woodland and taking her
at knife point, threatening to ruthlessly slash her
throat as he had her brother's. And her brother's
throat—Iain winced at the thought—had been
slashed from side to side; his head was nearly
severed. The very thought left his stomach sour.

Once Cameron was gone and they were alone

once more, Page opened her mouth to speak but then said nothing at all.

Iain felt he knew what she was thinking. "I'm certain he's merely preoccupied," he assured her.

His wife nodded, though her expression remained full of concern. "I'm certain, as well."

He took her by the shoulders and held her firmly, gazing reassuringly into her eyes. "There is little to be concerned about, wife. Broc is not the man they are looking for."

"Montgomerie swore to carve open the man's throat."

Iain nodded with certainty. "I canna blame him. The murderer deserves a judgment equal to the crime he committed."

But once again Page voiced Iain's own fear. "And if the murderer turns out to be one of our own? What then?"

Iain sighed heavily. "Then, in truth, I will be forced to relinquish him to Montgomerie," he said regretfully. "I cannot risk the amity of our clans for one man. Not even for Broc."

Page nodded but averted her gaze. "Well, I'm certain Broc has nought to do with any of it, anyway."

Iain bent and kissed her softly on the cheek, not wanting her to worry. "As am I," he affirmed. His gentle wife had formed an attachment to Broc. He knew she would fret until they discovered the murderer's true identity. As

would he. No man among them was more beloved than Broc Ceannfhionn.

In truth, Broc had never once considered his
own interests above those of the clan, and
though Page and Broc had not begun their acquaintance joyfully, Broc had been the first to
stand up for Page when his men had scorned
her.

Till the day he died, Iain would remain grateful to Broc for that.

His wife looked up at him, her beautiful eyes
beseeching, "And what do you intend to say to
Montgomerie?"

She worried at her lip, waiting for his response.

"Nought for now," he assured her and
winked, hoping to set her at ease as much as he
was able. He felt rather than heard her sigh.
" 'Tis hardly any of his affair where Broc lays his
head at night, dinna ye think?"

She smiled up at him, though reluctantly, and
nodded in accord. "Nor is it ours, in truth,
though my curiosity is surely piqued."

So was Iain's.

"Well, whoever she is, she must be quite spe-
cial. And, in fact, I must say 'tis about damned
time!" Page giggled, and he added, "There is
nought like a good woman to make a man feel
complete."

The worry lines vanished from her brow. She

smiled and then stood up on her tiptoes to kiss him tenderly upon the chin. A quiver raced down his spine, as ever it did at her merest touch. "Have I told you lately that I love you, Iain MacKinnon?"

"Aye, my lovely wife." He squeezed her gently, and his body stirred. "Broc will be fine," he assured her. "As for me . . ." He tugged at her arm and motioned her toward the stairs. "I willna be unless I might have a moment of your time."

She laughed. "Depraved, as I said," she told him with meaning, but she was the first to run to the stairs. "Last one upstairs has to be on bottom!"

Iain let her go ahead, unwilling to win this time.

Either way they both won, he acknowledged, as he lingered to watch her pert little derriere climb the staircase.

Damned if he didn't like being under that bottom!

Let her think she'd won.

Chapter 11

~~~⌒○○⌒~~~

Dust motes danced in the rays of sunlight that filtered in through the roof.

The first thing Elizabet came aware of was Broc's absence. Even before she sought him, she knew he wasn't there. Somehow, his presence filled a room, even in silence. His absence left it more gloomy than death.

He must have gone to speak with her brother, as he'd promised. And truth to tell, she was glad she didn't have to face him this morn.

She had invited his ardor. No matter how she wished to look at it, the fault was her own. If she hadn't first invited him to share her blanket, he would never have kissed her—and more. She had practically thrown herself into his arms, and her cheeks flamed with the memory. She had be-

haved shamefully. Now, how could she ever face
him again?

He was gone, and she wouldn't blame him if
he never came back.

What would she do if he refused to help her
now? What if it were true that Tomas wanted her
dead? Who would champion her if not Broc?
Who would even believe her?

Suddenly, everything had become so complicated.

Rising, she stretched the sleep from her limbs,
letting the blanket fall to the ground. And then
her gaze focused upon the threadbare cloth that
lay heaped at her feet. He'd returned the blanket
to her last night. The gesture moved her, though
she assured herself it didn't. She bent to retrieve
it and folded it, laying it upon the pallet, and
then went to the door, pushing the door open
somewhat warily.

In truth, she could seek out Piers on her own.
She was hardly helpless. And she certainly
hadn't come this far only to hide away for the
rest of her life. Not in shame and not in fear.

She would wait, indeed, but if he didn't return
soon, she would find her way alone.

The day was sunny and beautiful. A soft
breeze tousled her hair as she stepped into the
daylight, and she let the door close behind her.

What harm could come of her stepping out for
just a moment? She didn't intend to go far.

The forest was full of life. She could hear birds chirping in the trees and creatures scurrying as she passed. Out here, with the sun shining down upon her head, nothing seemed so terrible. When he returned, she would face him like a woman and not hide like a child.

What was done was done, and there was no way to rescind her actions.

Nor did she entirely wish to, if she would be honest with herself. In those moments she had felt more alive than she had ever felt in all her life. In fact, this morning, everything seemed somehow brighter, more vivid. Her senses were keener and her heart pounded with more vigor than she had ever felt before.

She took a deep breath and savored the moment of sweet purity.

This land was wild but truly beautiful. She could hardly fault the Scots for defending it so fiercely.

She stopped and turned to consider the hovel.

It was a simple dwelling, and its owner must have been a simple person. Unlike those women she'd grown accustomed to at court, this woman had lived entirely without luxuries. There was no extravagant bed upon which to lay her head. There were no kitchens, no corridors to be lost within, no gardens in which to brood.

But she had been free!

Completely and utterly free!

Had she been happy?

Had Broc visited her often?

Did they love each other?

Who was this man she had wed instead of Broc?

Her head filled with questions.

It was easier not to think about the bowman. She didn't wish to consider Tomas. Didn't want to think that her stepmother wished her dead. Whatever had she done to incur the woman's wrath? Surely Broc must be mistaken. He'd misunderstood the bowman's intent, that was all. Tomas had merely been defending her.

She tried to recall the previous day's events precisely. Her stepmother's brother hadn't been among her father's men—not when John had fallen and Broc had whisked her away. So, then, where had he been? And why hadn't he shown himself?

What would he have to gain by her death?

The question plagued her.

Broc would return soon enough with news.

In the meantime, she intended to take care of a few minor necessities. He couldn't possibly miss her in the short time she would be gone.

Broc had expected to find her still abed. Instead he returned to find her gone.

He tried not to panic—for her sake, not his own. He knew they were searching for her. What if they came across her in the woods? What if the bowman found her first? He'd promised her no harm would come to her, and he didn't intend to fail her now.

He barreled out of the hut, shoving the door open and calling her name frantically.

Christ, if they found her first, if they discovered his involvement, the clans would all be at war again. And he would be the man responsible for starting it. Was this how he repaid his debts to Iain?

God's truth, he would not allow it to come to that! He didn't know what he would do to stop it, but he damned well wouldn't be responsible for beginning a blood war worse than the MacLean-MacKinnon feud.

"Elizabet!" he called, running through the forest. And then at once he saw her, hiding behind a bush. Her head popped up, so he glimpsed only her eyes, and then she ducked once more.

She was hiding from him. She obviously didn't wish him to find her. Too bad. He had found her, and he bloody well intended to drag her back to the hut, will she nil she.

He picked up his pace and dove after her, determined to catch her. But he hardly expected what happened next.

Somehow, she seized hold of him, taking his arm and twisting his body in midair like some warrior woman. Dazed and confused, he landed with a thud on his back.

"Damn," he said, and groaned.

Elizabet stood, arms akimbo, and glared down at him. "What in damnation were you doing?"

He gave her a look of wounded pride and wounded feelings. "That hurt," he protested.

It served him right.

She raised a brow at him, unmoved by his little-boy pout. "I heard you the first time you called," she assured him. "Didn't it occur to you there might be a reason I didn't answer you at once?"

His confusion turned slowly to comprehension, and his gaze snapped to the place where she'd been stooped and then back to her. He seemed suddenly to realize what he'd interrupted, and his eyes widened. His cheeks began to color, and he rolled over onto his side, grunting in pain.

"It serves you well if you hurt yourself! How dare you burst upon me so rudely!"

He damned well ought to be as mortified as she was! "I'm fine," he said, rolling back toward her, holding his arm, nursing it, and looking sheepishly up at her.

"More's the pity!" How dare he look so beset when she had every right to chastise him!

"It's just that . . . I saw you were gone," he explained, wincing as he tried to rise.

"Am I a prisoner in that hovel? Can I not leave to attend to my own affairs when I must?"

He merely looked at her, blinking, looking boyishly innocent, but didn't reply.

"Well?" she persisted, vexed with herself for noticing, once more, the color of his eyes—the deepest blue she'd ever spied. "Am I your prisoner?" she demanded to know.

"Nay," he replied somewhat grudgingly, holding her gaze. Some strange light glittered there in the depths of his eyes. Admiration, mayhap? "I merely worried, lass."

"Aye, well, I have been taking care of myself since the day I was born," she informed him baldly. "I can certainly handle myself as long as it takes to—"

"Piss?"

Elizabet's face heated. Jesu, he didn't have to put it quite so crudely. "Let me see your arm!" she commanded him.

He offered it to her without pause, though smiling.

His mistake.

"Ouch!" he said when she seized it.

She didn't feel the least bit sorry for him!

And she didn't know how to remove his garment either. She wanted to be certain he hadn't hurt himself. "Take off your . . . gown," she commanded.

He shrugged away from her. "I'm fine."

"Of course you are, because you're a man and you're invincible," Elizabet argued. "Now, take it off!" When he didn't comply quickly enough, she took matters into her own hands, tugging at the garment to loosen it. Upon closer inspection, it was almost as though he'd just rolled himself up in one big piece of woolen cloth, and she grew frustrated at once. Surely there had to be some way to remove only the top portion of his clothing. "Haven't you people ever heard of needle and thread?"

He gave her a beleaguered look and once more tried to shrug free of her. "You people?"

"Well, I can't get it off!" Elizabet complained, giving up at last.

"I dinna wish ye to take it off. *We people* dinna run about showing our arses to strange women."

Impossible man.

Elizabet's cheeks warmed. "Well, I don't believe we are quite strangers after last night," she reminded him, a little offended.

"I beg to differ," he said, his eyes narrowing. "I've never met any woman stranger. One minute you like me, trust me, the next you loathe me!"

Elizabet's brows collided. "I never said I trusted you."

"Nay," he agreed. "Ye didn't." And he returned her wounded glance.

How dared he be offended!

"I only wanted to be certain you weren't injured."

He stared at her. And then suddenly his lips curved into a slow grin. "Verra well, then, have it your way." He stood with purpose, watching her intently, the muscles in his arms tensing. With merely a few tugs in the right places, the folds of cloth fell away, exposing him completely.

Her mouth fell open. For an instant, Elizabet merely stood, eyes wide.

Good Christ, every part of him was big.

His shoulders were massive and beautifully carved—like some majestic Roman statue. His chest seemed as solid as stone. His hips were lean and his legs so muscular that she could only stare in awe. Thin white scars covered his body—the most prominent a diagonal line across his breast. He was a man created for war, there was no doubt.

Her gaze fell to his male parts, conspicuous as it was.

Was he as equally created for love?

The thought occurred to her before she could keep it at bay. But it was a wicked, wicked thought, and she regretted allowing it audience at once.

Gasping softly at her own brazenness, she spun about, impatiently waving a hand, her face as hot as Hades must be. "Have it your way! You can get dressed now!"

He chuckled at her back. "But you haven't even looked at my arm yet," he protested.

God's truth, she had looked at more than enough!

She could hear the note of amusement in his voice, and she hardly appreciated it. "I'll look at it later!" she told him.

Another chuckle.

Sweet Mary, she tried to eradicate the image of his manhood from her memory, but it teased her, returning in glimpses to make her heart beat faster.

"Next time, respect my privacy!" she said, without turning. "You scared the—"

"Piss out o' ye?"

Elizabet gasped in outrage, turning to face him, her eyes wide with shock at his crudeness. "You have no manners at all!" she assured him.

"I never claimed to," he answered, throwing her own words back at her. "I'm a Scots barbarian, remember? *We people* are uncouth."

Guilt pricked at her.

"This all could have been avoided had you simply answered me," he rebuked her.

"I would have answered just as soon as I was finished—"

"Pissing?"

Elizabet tossed her hands upward. "Argh! I don't have to listen to this!"

"For all I knew," he continued to rebuke her as she walked away, "you could have been in danger and couldna call to me. I was merely trying to help."

"Well, I wasn't in the least danger, as you can see!" Except of wetting her shoes! She wiggled her toes, horrified by the discovery.

"Not this time," he argued.

The dampness on her feet renewed her ire.

She heard him chuckle softly at her back. "I do not find this the least amusing, I assure you!" she said without turning.

"What can I say?" he reasoned. "I'm a man. I'm easily amused."

Elizabet had no reply to that.

How could he remain so blithe when she was in a fit of temper? If she had not witnessed first hand his fury yesterday afternoon, she'd never have believed him capable of it. It was that everlasting mirth in his eyes that had made him appear so harmless. She didn't have to look to know he was watching her.

She started back in the direction from whence she'd come, contemplating her strange reaction to this man. Why did her heart beat so fast when he stared at her? And why was she so angry at him, despite the fact that he was only trying to help? So what if he'd kissed her, in truth. He'd

left her alone last night when she'd asked him
to, and she could hardly blame him for assuming
she was willing when she'd blatantly invited him
into her arms.

He was a threat to her somehow; he left her
feeling vulnerable. Something about him made
her yearn for more than the lonely life of a spin-
ster.

It was best to ignore the feelings he evoked in
her. She wanted her freedom. She didn't need a
man to tell her how and when to live her life.

"You're going the wrong way," he declared,
and the sound of his voice made her heart leap.

Elizabet turned to look at him. "Are you certain?" she asked him, growing flustered.

What was wrong with her?

And he was doing it again—making her dizzy,
muddling her mind with a simple look. She was
completely turned around. She studied the
woods then turned again to meet his amused
gaze.

"Verra certain," he replied. "I know these
woods well, Elizabet."

The intimate sound of her name upon his lips
made her breath catch. Nodding, she led the way
in the direction he indicated.

What are you doing? she asked herself. *Why
must you let every little thing he says and does affect
you so?*

What did it matter if he spoke her name so

gently that it made her think of a lover's whisper? *Don't think about him that way anymore*, she commanded herself.

How could she help it in his presence?

It was like closing one's eyes to the daylight and pretending the sun didn't shine though it beat down upon your head.

She heard his footfalls wane, so she turned to face him.

His face was screwed up as though in pain. She resisted the urge to run to him. It served him right if his arm hurt him. Mayhap next time he would think twice before he leaped over bushes to catch her. She set her hands upon her hips. "What's wrong now?"

"Nought. . . . 'Tis only that . . . well . . . if ye should need to . . ." His cheeks began to color as he gestured at the bush where he had first spied her. Elizabet's eyes widened as she waited for him to finish, horrified by what he was suggesting. "Finish," he said. "I could wait."

Elizabet's face heated. "Nay!" she exclaimed, and spun away from him. "I've no wish to show you my bare arse again, Scot!"

She walked faster, keenly aware that he followed, cursing him softly beneath her breath.

"Aye, but 'tis a beautiful arse," he commented, almost too low for her to hear him.

But she did hear him, and his tone betrayed no remorse at all.

Cad!

She didn't dare acknowledge his compliment. She kept marching, her cheeks flaming in chagrin. No man had ever given her such intimate flattery!

"In fact," he continued knavishly, " 'tis the most beautiful arse I have ever seen."

Elizabet's face suddenly felt as though it were a raging fire.

Jesu, what was she supposed to say to that?

It was on the tip of her tongue to ask just how many arses he had spied in his lifetime, but she held her tongue. Why should it matter to her if he had seen every arse from Edinburgh to London? It wasn't any of her affair if he'd bedded every woman he'd met.

He wasn't going to bed her!

Chapter 12

⁓◦◦⁓

The pain in Broc's arm was completely forgotten for the moment.

In fact, he was having a difficult time bringing himself to tell her that the hem of the back of her skirt was caught in the chain of her girdle.

He'd suggested she finish what he'd interrupted only so that she might readjust her skirts without him having to tell her that she was revealing herself. But now she was having such a pretty little fit of temper, and he wasn't certain how she would take it if he told her outright.

So he kept his mouth shut.

Besides, he was enjoying the view.

For her sake, he kept hoping her skirt would fall and cover that deliciously pert little arse, but it didn't, and he wondered after a time that she didn't feel the draft on her rear. He kept pace behind her, trying to keep his ardor cooled, but it wasn't easy when he kept imagining her stopping and bending to pick something up. What a beautiful sight that would be.

God's truth, he'd always had a weakness for women's arses, and this one was likely the sweetest arse he had ever beheld. His hands ached to ever so gently squeeze those firm cheeks. What he wouldn't give to have them fill his hands whilst she rode him.

How long had it been since he'd lain with a woman? He couldn't remember. He had always had far too much conscience to use a lass without promise of marriage.

Elizabet was different.

Despite his initial impression of her, he didn't believe her to be a courtesan. No woman of ill repute blushed so fiercely. Nay, 'twas a virgin's blush she wore. He'd watched her expressions carefully when he'd revealed himself to her, and it had been clear enough to Broc that she hadn't ever seen a man unclothed before. He was well endowed, to be certain, but not so much so as to deserve that look of absolute wonder on her face. The sight of him had for an instant struck her dumb. He might be flattered, in truth, but his pride was tempered by the knowledge that she was nought but an innocent. He felt all the more responsible for her.

In fact, if he had been any sort of gentleman,

and not a barbarian as she claimed, he probably wouldn't have been looking at that delightful bottom, but he couldn't look away.

Och, she had the most lovely little birthmark on her left cheek, perfectly formed, like a little half moon. It was nearly covered by her gown, but it kept peeking out at him from beneath as if it winked at him.

His loins tightened as he watched the delicate swing of her hips.

She was no frail little miss, either. He admired the way she had handled him so easily, tossing him to the ground with deft motions that had left him reeling. She wasn't a big woman, but neither was she small, and yet he had thought her puny simply because she was English.

That had been his first mistake.

His second was not telling her sooner that her sweet little bottom was causing him extreme discomfort.

His throat was growing parched. His lips felt as dry as baked mud. His blood sang with longing.

Was the hair on her mons as dark as the hair on her head?

Och, if she would merely bend over, he would know.

The very thought of her doing so made him dizzy.

He was only a man, he reasoned, and her

backside was tempting him beyond reason.

He tried to keep silent, not wanting to embarrass her, but his loins began to burn. Her firm little cheeks teased him to the point of torment, and his breath quickened with every step she took until it was nigh painful to breathe.

Self-preservation made him finally speak up, because he was going to go mad with desire if she didn't cover that delightful bottom.

Else he was going to do something he would later regret.

"And ye dinna worry," he assured her. "I promise never to tell anyone about that cute little mole."

She gasped aloud and spun to face him. "What mole?"

He winked at her. "That adorable half moon on your left cheek."

"Jesu!" she exclaimed, her hands instinctively going to her bottom. When she realized she was exposed, she shrieked in alarm and scrambled to release the gown from her girdle. "Oh, God! Oh, God!" Her cheeks flamed.

Broc couldn't suppress his grin. Despite the fire raging beneath his plaid, his good humor was more than restored. His shoulders shook with repressed laughter. Her pretty cheeks were so red they appeared painted.

She wouldn't look at him now, but merely worked fiercely to undo the skirt. "Why did you not tell me?"

"I did tell you," he pointed out.

"Hmph!" she exclaimed, still working fever-ishly to untangle her hem. She must have caught it when she'd lifted her gown, and then, when he'd interrupted her, she just hadn't noticed. He'd made her so bloody angry.

Elizabet cursed softly beneath her breath.

God's truth, if her hands hadn't been shaking so badly, she might have freed herself at once. Frustrated, she unfastened the girdle, jerking it away from her dress, letting the hem fall free. She replaced the girdle at once and tried to re-fasten it, her cheeks burning.

Sweet Jesu, he had been staring the entire time at her bottom! She was mortified! Yet she could hardly say anything in protest, when it wasn't his fault her arse had been exposed to God and all of creation!

Oh, the shame! She had been so bloody pre-occupied with her thoughts and her anger that she hadn't even noticed!

How was she supposed to face him now?

Just look into his eyes and pretend nothing hap-pened, she advised herself. After all, what was a body but flesh and bones? Her mother had bared hers to so many men Elizabet had lost count of those who had come and gone—and she had done so without the least shame. Not that Eli-zabet wished to bare herself to everyone who came along, but she couldn't help but admire her mother's dauntlessness. In truth, Elizabet secretly believed her mother had even reveled in her body, for she had been a beautiful woman. But she didn't dare really think of it too much. It was her mother, after all. Still, she could have used some of her mother's aplomb just now.

"I have a small mark on my right breast, too," she disclosed, pretending an indifference she didn't feel. "Care to see that, as well?"

When she dared to look up, he was smiling still.

The rogue!

"I'd be willing to suffer it," he replied, his eyes crinkling slightly at the corners.

Elizabet stood staring, at a loss for what to say next. Her eyes stung for an instant, so abashed did she feel. This was all too much for her. Her brother and Tomas and her dog . . .

And where was Harpy?

He must have sensed her distress. "Aw, come now, lass," he said. "Dinna fret. I'll show ye mine, if 'twill make you feel better."

He was teasing, she knew.

Her ire faded somewhat at his expression, warm as it was, though she didn't allow herself to smile. She didn't want to smile, though in truth, how could she remain angry when he had done no more than fill his eyes with what she had so brazenly revealed to him? Another man might have filled his hands, as well.

Elizabet had never met a man like Broc. He confused her more each moment she spent with him.

A little imp crawled into her for the briefest moment. She lifted her chin, challenging him. "Aye, show me!"

His brows lifted. "Are ye certain?"

"An eye for an eye!" she said, quoting scripture.

He gave her a lopsided smile. "And so ye wish to see my arse?"

Elizabet smirked, thinking mayhap he now regretted his offer. Too bad. "Bare it!" she challenged him.

He chuckled. "Verra well," he relented, and turned to show her his buttocks. He stood there a moment, looking awkward, and then with his good hand he reached back and lifted up his garment, showing her his bare arse.

Elizabet couldn't help herself. She began to giggle, though that didn't prompt him to cover himself. He waited patiently for her to finish.

"D'ye feel better yet?" he asked after a moment.

He flexed his cheeks and then released them, and Elizabet giggled harder. Her hand covered her mouth in absolute horror, though she didn't turn away.

Jesu, but it was a strong, muscular male arse.

And she had never seen a man's rear before. This one was hardly disappointing.

"Och, it sounds to me as though you feel better!"

Elizabet laughed outright.

"In fact, if I didn't know better, I would think ye were enjoying the view."

She was, in truth.

"Aye," she replied, when she could.

"Aye, ye feel better," he teased her, "or aye, you're enjoying the view?"

She wasn't about to admit to the latter. "Aye," she said, "I feel better!"

He dropped his plaid at last and turned around, his cheeks flaming, though his eyes revealed only mirth.

His gesture warmed her. He scarce knew her. So why should he care how she felt?

She screwed up her face at him, confused. "Why are you so kind to me?"

He returned to coddling his injured arm but only stared into her eyes.

"Is it your habit to play knight in shining armor for every woman you meet?"

Broc continued to stare at her, considering her question.

In truth, it wasn't.

But it was his habit to protect those he loved.

Even with Page, though her father had rebuffed her, he hadn't felt the least compelled to champion her—not at the beginning. In fact, simply because of her birth, he had felt driven to protect Iain from her. And when Iain had taken her under his wing, Broc had felt angry. Page had had to prove herself to him before he accepted her. Until then, he'd been more than willing to simply set her free so that she could find her way to wherever she cared to go—it hadn't mattered to him, so long as she wasn't a threat to his kinsmen.

So why, in truth, did he feel so obligated to protect Elizabet when she had the potential to devastate not merely his own clan, but the peace of many.

He had no answer to that question.

"Nay," he said at last.

"So why are you helping me?"

He gave her a pointed look. "Was I supposed to let the man shoot you before my verra eyes?"

She shook her head, looking dejected, as though it were not the answer she wished to hear.

Broc wanted suddenly to take her into his arms and gently hold her. He wanted to tell her everything would be fine.

He wanted to kiss her.

Christ, was he jeopardizing his entire clan for his own desires? Would he have done the same had Elizabet been a man—an Englishman at that?

He didn't think so. Unsettled by his own questions, he squeezed his arm and winced in pain.

She came toward him at once. "At least allow me to return the favor by tending your arm."

"There is nought wrong with my arm!" he said, with far more vehemence than he'd intended.

She stopped in her tracks, casting her arms up in offense. "Fine! Be stubborn and enjoy your pain!"

He scowled at her. "I've endured far worse."

She spun about and marched away. "Of course," she countered. "Because you're a man!"

Without another word, she hurried along the path ahead of him, and he started after her, muttering to himself, "Damned woman!"

God's truth, he'd rather have a dog.

Piers' mood was sour, to say the least.

They'd searched the entire perimeter of his property and had found no sign of his cousin's daughter. He was done for the afternoon, but that didn't mean her well-being didn't weigh heavily upon his mind. How in bloody damnation had he been embroiled in this situation without warning?

"Why the hell did Geoffrey send his children without asking me first?" he snapped at Tomas as he dismounted in the courtyard.

Tomas shrugged as he dismounted from his

own horse and handed his reins to a stable boy.
"He is hardly the brightest man," Tomas remarked.

That much was true, Piers accepted, though it
annoyed him that Tomas would say so. Geoffrey
had, in fact, had ample opportunity to advance
himself but had chosen to rely on his wives'
dowries to support him. And now he was wedding someone else. Who was this woman anyway? Piers had a sense that it was her fault these
young people were endangered. Geoffrey might
have been shiftless, but he certainly wasn't so
cold as to throw his own children out of his
home. Piers didn't like this new bride already—
nor did he particularly like her emissary brother.

He eyed the man speculatively as they made
their way toward the hall. There was something
about the lad that set his teeth on edge—his
manner, perhaps. His arrogance was offensive,
and furthermore his lack of emotion over John's
death was suspicious. And his anger over Elizabet's disappearance seemed somehow con-
trived and empty.

Elizabet. Poor woman. Though he hadn't
asked to be her guardian, Piers would feel responsible if she was harmed. As it was, he felt
no small amount of guilt over John's death. He
could have at least met them at the border and
given them safe passage—if only he had known
they were coming.

God's teeth, hadn't his cousin realized that these lands were full of strife still? These were perilous times even for native clans but particularly so for an outlander. Damn! Hadn't Geoffrey realized that was why Piers had been sent here? It had been his objective to penetrate these people, to befriend them if possible, and to unite them with England by force if need be—a duty to which he no longer felt entirely committed.

These Highlanders had earned his highest respect. They were a fiercely loyal people, who protected their clansmen without reservation. That he'd accomplished some manner of peace between them was less a tribute to his fighting skills, for which he'd been chosen initially, and more a matter of God's intervention. He'd fallen in love with the most beautiful woman in all of Scotia. She just happened to have a very influential family.

"If Elizabet is not found, Geoffrey will not rest until her death is avenged!" Tomas declared pompously.

They entered the hall, and Meghan ran toward them, her expression full of concern. When she reached Piers, he embraced her and bent to kiss her upon the cheek. "We found nought at all," he told her, ignoring Tomas's bluster.

The man was beginning to annoy him heartily.

With his arm about Meghan's shoulder, he turned to address Tomas. "And what makes you presume Elizabet dead?"

He seemed startled by the question, non-plussed. "John is dead," he replied, as though that were portent.

Piers nodded soberly. John was, indeed, dead—poor little fellow. The slit in his throat was wider than the English Channel. Whoever had sliced it hadn't intended him to survive.

Meghan's voice was fretful. "I cannot imagine that someone would simply murder a helpless woman!"

It seemed to Piers that Tomas sneered in response. "You are such an innocent, demoiselle! There are men out here who would slice Eliza-bet's throat just as readily as they would any man's."

Meghan winced, casting Piers a worried glance.

"Have you not heard the tales of brutal rape and murder?" Tomas continued, offering evi-dence.

Meghan looked up at Piers as she shook her head.

"As a matter of fact," Tomas continued, "just before I left England, a young girl was discov-ered in the forest near Geoffrey's keep, her body broken and desecrated, discarded after being ruthlessly used."

"How dreadful!" Meghan exclaimed.

"Her tongue had been snipped out so that she could not call out for help."

Meghan gasped and seized hold of Piers' arm.

"Aye, 'tis true!" Tomas declared, watching her far too keenly.

He was distressing her, and God's truth, Piers thought he might even be enjoying it.

"In fact," Tomas persisted, and Meghan squeezed Piers' arm in silent appeal, "she was—"

"That's quite enough," Piers said, hugging his wife a little closer in order to ease her fears. He smiled tolerantly at the man, not wishing him to take offense, for Geoffrey's sake. Else, in truth, Piers might have made him sleep in the barn.

At every bloody turn, Tomas had dominated the search efforts, though he couldn't possibly have any notion where best to hunt. Piers had humored him only because he'd known his own men would pay him little deference. Still, the day had taken its toll upon Piers, and he was ready for a tankard of ale and his lovely wife's attentions.

The day had been long and would grow longer still.

"If you will excuse us." Piers bowed slightly to excuse himself.

"Of course," Tomas yielded, and without another word Piers ushered his wife away from their unwanted visitor.

"You are squeezing my arm!" Meghan complained beneath her breath.

Piers released her, unaware that he was hurting her. "I'm sorry, my darling."

"What is wrong?"

Piers twined his hand into her hair as they walked, loving the silky feel of it. "Nought, my love. It's just been a harrowing day."

She nodded, understanding, and reached out to hold his hand, casting a casual glance back as she did so. "I dinna believe I like that man verra much," she confessed in a whisper when they were far enough from Tomas.

He pulled her toward the stairs that led to their chamber, wanting a little privacy before the evening meal.

"Och, my love, you look verra weary," she said, turning to embrace him at the foot of the staircase.

Piers held her. "I am," he replied. "Weary and confused." She squeezed him, comforting him. "Christ, did Geoffrey think I would deny him? Did he think I would turn his children away? Why did he not send word to me so that I could give them safe passage?"

She laid her head upon his chest, hugging him. "I dinna know, my darling."

Their deaths would weigh heavily upon his shoulders. He had to find Elizabet, no matter if he had to search for her clear to Edinburgh and beyond. How would he send word to Geoffrey that both his youngest children had perished even before they had reached safe harbor?

John, Piers had remembered from his youth. That face hadn't changed very much, and to see it in death had wrenched at his heart. The little boy John had been once upon a time had followed Piers about, admiration writ upon his face, awe in his voice, and desire to earn his father's approval so strong that it was plain even to Piers, who visited scarce at all.

He sighed heavily. "Did you manage to set the funeral for tonight?"

Meghan looked up at him, her eyes full of compassion. "Tomorrow, and Gavin will come to give a short sermon."

Piers nodded. He didn't really care personally whether the grave was blessed or not, but Geoffrey would.

He reached down to touch his wife's cheek and couldn't help himself. He took her face into his hands and then bent to kiss her. "Thank you," he whispered.

"Whatever for?"

He smiled softly at her, wanting her to realize how grateful he was for her love. "For coming into my life."

She returned the smile and reached up to touch his lips. "Och, husband, tonight you will be cursing me for the same when you see what I have done with the chapel."

Piers slanted her a look. "What chapel?"

She grinned up at him and then turned to climb the stairs. "The one we have been building for Gavin," she disclosed, but didn't turn. She hurried up before him.

Piers stood, confused, at the bottom of the stairs. "What do you mean? What chapel have we been building for Gavin?"

She wouldn't turn around, continuing up the stairs.

"Meghan!" he thundered, and started up after her. "We haven't been building any chapel for Gavin!"

She tossed her hair from her face as she reached the top of the stairs and looked down at him. "Oh, but we have! It was going to be a surprise!"

God's teeth, he really didn't want to have to listen to her brother's sermons every time he turned around!

"It will give him such joy," she declared. "He has nobody, Piers, and I wanted to give him something to live for. He must be so lonely now that Colin and Leith are both wed, as well!"

Piers rolled his eyes.

"I have been waiting to tell you, but what better time. 'Twill be perfect for John's service. Are you angry, my love?"

He stood there, shaking his head, thinking of all the lies he would have to tell in order to miss her brother's sermons. If his past deeds hadn't earned him a cozy place in hell, his future ones surely would!

She was looking at him so dejectedly.

How could he possibly be angry with her?

"Damn, woman!" he exclaimed and started again up the stairs after her. "I'm going to have to paddle that delightful arse of yours!"

She shrieked in alarm and ran away in the direction of their room, and Piers smiled to himself as he heard her giggle and slam the door behind her.

He would never touch her in anger, she knew, and the door would never be locked against him. No man worthy of the name would ever harm a woman. But truth to tell, he couldn't wait to get his hands on his wife's lovely arse.

It would be the one bright spot of his day.

Damn Tomas and Geoffrey, both! He wasn't about to feel the least bit guilty about taking five moments of pleasure with the woman he loved.

Chapter 13

"There is nought wrong with your arm," Elizabet announced, still perturbed, though in truth more with herself than she was with him.

Broc sat patiently at the little table while she tended him, and his forbearance only set her more on edge. He was covered with the blanket, but the simple knowledge that he was bare beneath it was enough to make her breath catch painfully.

He peered up at her, lifting a surly brow, and said, "I tried to tell you, woman, but you wouldn't listen."

"Well, you were right."

He smiled up at her, winking, and assured her, "I dinna break verra easily."

"I see that," she replied, and smiled back.

171

For an instant, they merely stared at each other, and Elizabet's heart began to beat softly against her breast. "At any rate, I wish to thank you."

"For what?"

His gaze seemed to hold her. She couldn't look away. "For all that you've done for me."

"Och, lass, but I've done nothing more than any man would have."

Mayhap it was true, but Elizabet had not known that sort of man. Not even her father had really had any use for her. He was kind, to be sure, but he'd certainly never sacrificed anything for her sake. And when she'd become a burden, he'd sent her away.

Uncomfortable with the feelings she was experiencing, she averted her gaze, peering down at his hands upon the table. Big hands. Gentle hands. The sight of them made her breath quicken. Those hands had touched her intimately. They had caressed her where no man had ever dared.

"What is it, Elizabet?"

She shook her head, her throat thickening. "Nought. . . . It's simply that no one has ever championed me before—save my brother John," she amended. "He didn't have to but he did, even though it caused him grief from my other brothers and sisters."

Broc knit his brows. "I dinna understand. Why

should it have caused him grief?" He could not even begin to imagine how it must feel to have a large family with so many siblings. That any should reject another was unthinkable.

"Well, you see . . . I did not know any of them until I was already grown." She cast him an anxious glance. "My mother was a leman, you see, a mistress. She raised me alone. I did not even know my father until a few years ago. He took me in after my mother died."

He was quiet a long moment and then disclosed, "I understand what 'tis like to be alone."

And somehow, as she peered into his eyes, she understood that he did.

They were kindred spirits.

Broc had never spoken to anyone of his circumstances, not even to Colin, who was his best friend, or Iain, who was like his brother.

She glanced up at him, her heart in her eyes, and he wanted suddenly to take her into his arms and hold her, comfort her.

He recognized something in her, something that spoke to him instinctively, something that told him they were very much alike. It wasn't anything he could put his finger on, but something there, nonetheless.

"You have no brothers or sisters?" she asked him.

Broc shook his head. "Nor mother nor father. They were all murdered." *By your people*, he nearly added. "When I was but a lad." His anger resurfaced just in the telling, but he reminded himself that she was not responsible for his mother's death. She had nought to do with it.

And the look she gave him tempered his rage, so deep was the compassion he spied in her eyes.

Still he could not speak of this, not even with her. "It was a long time ago," he said, refusing to speak of it more. "And I've a good family and many friends." He was fortunate, he told himself. Many had not even that.

Find ye a good woman to cherish and give her strong bairns. Let your father's blood live long in your veins and those of your children! You are the last of the MacEanraig clan, lad.

Auld Alma's voice whispered in his ear.

He stared at Elizabet, his heart hammering.

She looked away. "Have you . . . a wife, then?" she asked, sounding dejected at the mere possibility.

Broc blinked at the question.

Wife?

"Nay."

She lifted her gaze, a sudden smile hidden in her eyes, and somehow her hopeful expression lifted his mood.

"Though, God's truth, as long as I had my dog I never suffered a cold bed."

"Dog!" She shrieked with laughter.

He laughed along with her and pretended a

serious tone, "Aye, well, who needs a bloody wife when ye can have a dog?"

Her hand went to her mouth, though she failed to hold in her laughter.

He winked at her.

"Och, think about it, lass. A dog never grouses when ye come home late, nor does she care if ye bed a wench or two while you're away. She's pleased so long as ye bring her home a bone."

"Oh, my!" She laughed softly and the sound of it sent an unexpected shudder through him.

Her face fairly glowed. Christ, but she was lovely, more lovely every instant that he knew her.

She arched a perfectly formed brow and lifted a hand to her thick plait, toying with it nervously, her smile brilliant. God, but he wished she would undo it again so he could see the true length of her hair. Last night it had felt so soft in his hands. Her mouth had tasted so sweet. He found himself thirsting for another ambrosial sip.

"So you're one of those?" she asked him coyly, eyeing him reproachfully.

He grinned. "One of which?"

"One of those who keeps a woman in every town he visits." She nodded once with comprehension. "My mother knew many such men."

"No women," he assured her, with another teasing wink. It felt so good to banter with her. "But certainly a dog in every town."

She laughed softly and glanced down at the crucifix she wore, her expression suddenly wistful.

"What is it, lass?"

She turned a somewhat melancholic smile up at him. "It feels good to laugh. In truth, 'tis been a long, long time since I've felt such ease with someone," she confessed. "I've sorely missed it."

Who else had she shared that beauteous smile with?

Broc's gut churned over the possibilities. He didn't want her heart to belong to anyone else.

She gripped her plait and stared, transfixed, as though lost in memory.

Was she remembering some lover who had cherished her once upon a time?

His body roused at the ardor visible in her eyes, no matter that it was not for him.

He wanted that look to be for him.

Aye, he wanted his woman to desire his body, but he hadn't realized how much he'd craved that gentle, precious glance until he'd spied it in Elizabet's eyes.

She began to fiddle with the bindings of her plait, pulling at the golden ribbon, and the shimmering material was a reminder that she was not for him. She was not of his ilk. She had been born to a world of riches and luxuries, while he had been raised in the dirt.

What did he have to give her but his body?

His father had been chieftain of their clan, but his true kinsmen were all dead and buried now. He had no coffers of his own to share with her, nor, in truth, even the right to offer sanctuary. He was risking much to help her—much that wasn't his own.

Guilt pricked at him.

Still, he wasn't about to walk away.

Something inside urged him to stay.

Before he could stop himself, he reached out and seized her hand, clutching her fingers from which the crucifix dangled, pulling her nearer.

Elizabet gasped in surprise.

"Whose memory do I behold in your eyes?" he demanded to know.

For an instant, she didn't answer, and he thought she would refuse him an answer. He tugged on the crucifix.

"M-my mother," she stammered at last.

Her hand gripped the cross more firmly, but she didn't resist him. "This was hers," she revealed. "She wore it always."

He wanted to kiss her, desperately craved her mouth, but the memory of last eve held him at bay.

Elizabet suddenly couldn't breathe. Her heart fluttered at the intensity of his gaze.

He made no further advances, merely stared, tugging softly at the crucifix.

Some part of her prayed he would kiss her

now. Some other part of her screamed in fear.

But fear of what?

Fear of losing her freedom.

Fear of losing her heart.

He glanced down to inspect the crucifix and then back up into her eyes.

"It was a gift to my mother," she disclosed. "And she gave it to me before she died."

He continued to stare at her, his eyes gleaming strangely. "Beautiful," he said softly.

Elizabet felt her legs go weak beneath her. She swallowed convulsively as he tugged once more on the crucifix. Sheer will kept her from tumbling into his lap.

She held her breath, waiting . . . anticipating.

"Did no one ever tell you how beautiful you are?" he said softly.

Elizabet's entire body quivered at his words. She shook her head, her heart beating more furiously still, her lips feeling suddenly parched as he continued to stare into her eyes. She wetted her lips with her tongue, watching his expression intently.

His eyes never left hers.

He tugged a little harder on the crucifix, drawing her down, and Elizabet found she hadn't the will to resist. If he kissed her, she would not protest.

She fell to her knees before him, and he released the crucifix at last. To her mortification, it swung down against her body, tapping gently at her most private place, that place where his fingers had caressed her. Her gaze snapped up to meet his, and her chest squeezed painfully at the hunger apparent in his expression. His gaze flicked down for an instant at the swinging cross and then back up as it continued to tap against her insistently.

She swallowed convulsively.

God's truth, he was no longer touching her at all, but every nerve in her body came alive as she looked into his eyes . . . as the crucifix teased her . . . as she imagined his finger touching her there instead . . . as she remembered his kiss, his touch.

God forgive her for her wicked thoughts! In truth, she was worse than her mother, because she was a wanton without noble cause. Her mother, at least, had been able to claim her daughter's best interests.

Her hand fell upon his thigh, and she was keenly aware of his nakedness beneath the blanket. The images that accosted her made her skin flush with heat.

He lifted a hand to her nape, tangling his fingers gently into her hair. Shivers raced down her spine.

"Y-you should dress now," she proposed, trying to find some measure of reason amidst the insanity of her thoughts.

"Should I?" he asked her, his voice husky. And then, "What if I dinna wish to?"

Elizabet shuddered softly at his words.

Jesu, she wasn't entirely certain she wished him to either. She wanted to see him, all of him. He was beautiful in a way no man had ever been. He was tall and strong and his skin seemed so soft and yet so hard. She wanted more than anything to reach out and touch his arm, to feel the ripples in his sinewy flesh.

She wanted to kiss him again, wanted to feel the delicious weight of him bearing down against her.

He watched her, his eyes slitting with desire, and Elizabet wasn't so naive that she didn't understand the turn of his thoughts.

Hers had gone there as well.

" 'Tis a lovely crucifix," he murmured, and bent nearer, closing the unfathomable distance between their mouths. It seemed to Elizabet that he hovered so near . . . so blissfully near . . . but so very, very far.

She would never have the nerve to crane her neck upward, to touch her lips to his. She could never be so bold as to kiss a man. But, sweet Mary, she wanted to.

In that instant, there was nothing she had ever yearned for more.

Again she swallowed.

"My m-mother never made any apologies for

who she was," she said, trying to find suitable conversation, though her throat was almost too parched to speak. She was rambling, she realized, but couldn't help it. Her heart was beating so fiercely that she thought she would swoon. "She did what she pleased and chose to live frugally so that she might leave everything to me. I never realized at the time how much she gave up for me, but so much became clear after her death. I miss her desperately."

She could feel the warmth of his breath on her face; his lips hovered so near. "So she left you her coffers?"

"Aye," Elizabet replied, and smiled as she said, "Though 'tis hardly enough to compensate a man for having to bear with me."

His eyes seemed to twinkle at her self-deprecating jest. "Because you're so damned contrary?" he said.

Elizabet laughed softly at the way he said it—warmly and without enmity. "It does seem I have inherited more than my mother's coffers," she confessed, unwilling to remove her hand from his leg. It was far too bold, she realized, and she was tempting his will, but she couldn't help herself. She gathered the blanket in her fist, clutching it breathlessly. "She was . . . a strong woman, you see."

"Was she?" he asked and bent a little closer.

Elizabet shut her eyes, praying for the touch

of his lips. God, she wanted this so desperately.

And then suddenly her eyes flew open with the realization of what it was that Tomas would have to gain with her death. "My dowry!"

He blinked at her, confused by her outburst. "What?"

"Jesu! Why did I not realize sooner! My dowry!" she declared. "That's what Tomas is after!"

He narrowed his eyes at her, not understanding.

"You see, my father insisted I take it with me to give to Piers so that Piers might use it to make me a better match. Only Tomas, John and I knew of it, lest greed tempt the others. But 'tis hardly enough to kill a man over." She shook her head, contemplating the absurdity of it.

Broc shook his head as he told her, "Some men would kill simply for a morsel of food, lass. How much were ye carrying and where is it now?"

"A pouch full of jewels and coins," Elizabet revealed. "John held it for me."

He seemed to consider her disclosure, and his brows knit as he asked her. "Ye say John held it?"

Something like dread crept through her at his tone, at his look. She nodded. What if Tomas intended to be rid of them both? What if he had already killed John? "Oh, God . . . Broc . . . are you certain my brother was unharmed?"

He didn't answer.

Elizabet's heart flip-flopped painfully.

He averted his eyes for the briefest instant, then said to her with absolute certainty. "When last I saw your brother, Elizabet, he was in danger of suffering no more than a headache. I tell you, he *was* fine."

Elizabet knit her brows. "You must go to him, Broc, and beg him to come to me, so I can tell him what we suspect! I cannot bear to think that something may happen to him before we can speak with Piers!"

His jaw clenched, and he appeared distraught at her behest.

"Please!" Elizabet begged him, thinking mayhap he didn't wish to leave her unprotected. "I swear I will stay out of trouble until you return. I promise to wait inside and take no chances! I give you my word!"

He reached out and gently touched her cheek with a finger, startling her with the tender touch.

Elizabet's breath caught at the tenderness of the gesture. For a long moment, he held her gaze, saying nothing, and in that instant she chanced to spy his heart in his eyes.

No one had ever looked at her that way—so sincerely, so full of genuine concern.

She trusted him. She did. The realization brought tears to her eyes. She knew without doubt he meant only to help her, and her heart swelled with gratitude.

Words stuck in her throat. There was nothing she could say that would reveal her appreciation.

But there was something she could do.

Somehow, she would repay him for his kindness.

Chapter 14

⌒◦◯◯◦⌒

The lie had become his own cross.

He couldn't tell Elizabet her brother was dead, but with every lie he spoke, another nail was driven deep into his soul.

That look in her eyes, that trust she had placed in him, weighed heavily upon him now. He couldn't keep the truth from her forever. He knew that. Soon she would have to know, but he wanted to be certain she would no longer be in danger once he let her go.

She would loathe him, he realized.

As soon as the words left his lips, she would never again look at him that way. He dreaded that moment more than he'd ever dreaded anything in his life.

What was he supposed to do now?

She wanted him to speak to her brother, to

bring him to her. How was he going to manage another lie without Elizabet discovering the truth?

And where the hell was he supposed to go now? Certainly not to Piers. But he needed to confide in somebody. Not Iain—he couldn't involve Iain. Not Colin—he couldn't place Colin in such an untenable position. Nor Seana—he couldn't ask her to lie to her new husband.

Christ, never in his life had he felt so alone.

If he left Elizabet now and confided in Iain, he knew Iain would take his side, but he couldn't just hand Elizabet over to her murderer. It was Broc's word against Tomas's, and who would believe him?

Not Elizabet.

And God's truth, that seemed to be the only thing that mattered.

For now, Elizabet was safe enough in the hut. No one could tell her anything so long as no one knew where she was. He just needed to be certain Seana would not stumble upon her.

And with that in mind he decided to pay a little visit to the newlyweds.

"Do ye realize we've no' had five moments together alone since before the wedding?" Colin Mac Brodie complained to his wife when they were behind closed doors at last.

"Aye, my darling, but 'tis all for good cause. Poor woman!" she declared.

It was her first time in Colin's chambers. She'd remained with Meghan until their nuptials and then had spent her wedding night under Montgomerie's roof, as well. Tonight, for the first time, Colin had brought her home, and she looked curiously about the room he called his own, examining all he had chosen to surround himself with—the most apparent, an elaborate bed, which raised her brows at first sight. It was obvious what importance he gave the single piece of furniture, for it was ornately carved and polished to a shine. She cast him a chiding glance, and he seemed to understand precisely what she was thinking.

"I have never brought any woman here," he assured her. I had that bed built for you and me."

"Truly?" She peered back at him, both surprised and moved by the gesture.

"My wedding gift to you," he disclosed, and smiled that brilliant Colin smile she so adored. Only her husband could manage to look so blessed mischievous and innocent at once.

He came up behind her as she stood running her fingers over the soft blankets that covered the oaken monstrosity. "My beautiful wife," he whispered at her ear.

" 'Tis lovely, Colin."

"*You* are lovely," he countered, embracing her tightly. Like a wee child hugging his favorite toy, he squeezed and rocked her gently. But then his hands wandered to her breasts, and he squeezed softly, sucking in a breath in appreciation.

Seana laughed at his play.

"Och, but I love your body, woman!"

She loved his, as well, and she reached back to tweak him where she knew he would most appreciate it.

"Wicked wench!"

"I intend to remove every memory of every woman from your mind, Colin Mac Brodie!"

He chuckled at her threat and tickled the back of her neck with his tongue. "What women?" he murmured, and she turned in his arms to face him.

She arched a brow. "You know verra well what women we are speaking of."

"You are the only woman for me, wife."

Seana tilted him a coy glance, enjoying his attentions. She knew he spoke the truth, but she still wanted to hear it from his lips again and again—and again.

"The only woman?"

He kissed her again with meaning, closing his eyes. "Aye, my love."

"And there aren't any other women still on your mind?"

"Hmm . . ." He opened his eyes suddenly, "Well, mayhap there is just one."

Seana gasped at his candid reply.

"Wretch!"

He laughed and pushed her back upon the soft bed, then pounced on her, pinning her beneath him.

Seana pushed at his chest. "Get off me, you brat!"

He grinned down at her. "You ask me an honest question, my dear, you get an honest answer."

Seana narrowed her eyes at him, hardly thinking him amusing. "Who?" she demanded.

He wiggled his brows at her and pushed his pelvis against her, teasing. "You really wish to know?"

Seana glared up at him. "Aye!" He opened his mouth to speak. "Nay!"

Laughing, he seized her about the waist and rolled so that she sat atop him. "Silly wench! God's truth, the only other woman I have on my mind is Piers' cousin."

Seana sighed in relief. "Och! You could have said so!"

"I did say so," he protested. "You asked, wife, and I answered."

She gave him a pretty pout. "You knew what I meant."

His gaze turned sober then, and he curled his

hand about her nape. "Believe me when I tell you, Seana, from this moment forward, no woman exists for me but you."

She kissed him again, sighing with contentment. "I do love you, Colin."

"I know," he replied with a roguish grin, and Seana could only smile at his cocky answer. He was absolutely intolerable, her husband, but she loved him fiercely—everything about him from his wicked smile to his unmanageable arrogance. She plopped herself down upon the bed beside him, staring at the ceiling.

They had searched again all day but had found no sign of the poor woman. Everyone had been shocked by the abduction, and the clans had all united in their efforts to find the girl. It was a heartwarming sight to see, Montgomerie riding with the Brodies, and the MacKinnons had joined them, as well.

"Will you search again tomorrow?" she asked.

He slid a hand beneath her back and lay beside her, staring at the ceiling as well. He sighed heavily, and she understood his sentiments precisely. She wanted him at her side as well, but if it were she who was missing, she would like to think everyone would do the same for her.

"Aye." He turned to her then, holding her close. "I don't know what I'd do if I lost you," he said.

Seana reached out to brush the hair from his

face. It was the most beautiful face she'd ever seen, and she never tired of looking at him. "You will never lose me," she promised.

"Seana," he said, sounding distressed at the possibility. "It took me a lifetime to find you again, and I vow I'll never let anyone harm you!"

She smiled at him, hoping he could see the love in her eyes. "I know that, my darling."

Something thumped twice against the window, the sound, like two strikes of a small stone, distinct enough to distract them both.

Colin looked up at the window with narrowed eyes. "What the hell was that?"

Seana cast a wary glance at the window.

"Damned cats!" her husband said, evidently deciding it was her father's cats. "I swear to God they seem to know precisely when to appear. If I didn't know better I would think their presence was deliberate!"

She looked at him. "Colin," she said, "cats don't knock!"

He pushed himself off the bed. "You've a point." He was halfway to the window when the thump sounded once more. "I've waited all day for this moment. Whoever is out there had better have a damned good reason to be rapping at our window!"

Seana smiled at his use of the word "our" and watched him tear open the shutters with a vengeance. She felt sorry for whoever was calling on them. Just for an instant, she worried it might be one of his old lovers, despite his assurance that he'd never brought any to his own bed. But no one would disrespect her so, not on the second night of her nuptials, and she had every faith that if anyone did, her husband would set things straight.

Colin peered down into the courtyard, leaning over the sill to better see into the darkness. She knew at once when he began to curse who it was that stood down below.

"You damned whoreson bastard!" he barked. "I dinna see you all day when your arse was needed most, and you show up when I'm about to enjoy my wife!"

Seana's face heated at the implication. She told herself it was only Broc, but it still embarrassed her. Men were crude—they just didn't seem to be able to help it, and these two were insufferable together. She had long ago resigned herself to that.

"What the hell do you want?" Colin railed at Broc.

"I didn't realize how late it was," Broc shouted in apology.

His tone seemed overly somber, and Seana knew something must be wrong.

"I figured you'd had more than enough time with Seana, you damned gorger, and I wanted to ask you about the search efforts."

"I'll never have enough of my wife," Colin assured Broc, and that, too, brought a smile to Seana's lips. "Find yourself a good woman and quit sleeping with mangy dogs, and you'll understand what I mean."

Seana could hear Broc's husky laughter drift up through their window, but it was strained and lacked his usual fervor. She wondered what had brought him here so late.

"'Tis a mean blow," Broc proclaimed, "as I have no more dog, no woman, and no longer any friend since he's gone and gotten himself wed!"

Colin shouted down at him, "Bloody right, you sorry bastard! Come calling when that bright yellow sphere is in the sky, and I might not be so ornery!"

"You're always ornery," Broc argued.

Seana rose from the bed, adjusting her skirts, giving her husband a warm glance. She could still scarce believe he was her husband now, that she was duly wedded to him and would share his life. God had surely blessed her. "I'll go see if Alison has ale on hand."

Colin turned to wink at her. "I love you, wench."

It was Seana's turn to give the cocky response. A secret smile turned the corners of her mouth. "I know."

He laughed, and then pointed a finger at her accusingly and said, "Dinna even think you'll come back up and go to sleep without me, wife. I intend to make you sit right at my side."

"Who, me?" she asked immodestly and lifted her skirt playfully, teasing him with a glimpse of what he could not have at that instant. "Never!" she proclaimed, and hurried to the door, giggling, when he took a step toward her.

"Wicked wench," he muttered, and turned again to the window as she left the room. "I'll be down in a damned moment!" he told his long time friend. "To strangle you with my bare hands!"

Chapter 15

◦◦◦◦◦

Colin knew something was wrong.

It wasn't like Broc just to show up and throw stones at his window. In fact, he didn't think either of them had done any such thing since they had been children together. He hurried down the stairs and opened the door, allowing Broc entrance. He looked weary and apprehensive, almost as though he regretted his visit.

"Seana's gone after ale. So tell me, what brings you here so late, my friend?"

Broc scraped his boots on the doorsill before entering, leaving behind a thick sheet of peat and mud. "I heard the rumors upon my return ... about the Sassenach wench gone missing. I came to see what you knew."

Broc closed the door behind him, and Colin

led the way into the hall, talking as he went. "Not verra much," he said. "She's a distant cousin of Piers, though it seems he didn't even realize she was coming. He was furious she crossed the border with such inadequate escort."

The restrained anger in Broc's voice was unmistakable. "I, too, wondered why the bloody hell they sent a woman essentially alone!"

Colin lifted his brows at the fervent declaration. "It seems her father feared Montgomerie would turn down his request to take them into his wardship and didn't wish to give Piers the opportunity. He sent the girl along with her brother, escorted by his brother-in-law and three men. Come, sit down," he commanded his friend.

Broc hesitated, and Colin turned to face him. "Are you certain 'tis alright?" Broc asked.

Colin chuckled with genuine good humor. "Now you think to ask?" He reached out and slapped Broc upon the back. "Get your arse in here and stay a while."

A grin tugged at Broc's mouth. "If you insist, my friend."

"I do," Colin assured him, and turned again to lead the way to the high table. He took his seat and offered Broc the one across from him.

"So how is wedded life?" Broc asked him as he sat.

Colin's grin widened. "I wouldn't know yet—

between missing wenches and discourteous friends."

Broc seemed to sober at that remark.

"I was jesting," Colin assured him.

Broc nodded, though still somber. It was unlike him to be so staid, and Colin leaned forward in his chair, resting his elbows upon the table as he regarded his friend.

"You know I wouldn't have come—" Broc began.

"I do know," Colin assured him, becoming concerned. "What is it?"

"I canna say precisely, and it would serve us both better if ye dinna ask."

"I see."

Broc hadn't intended to reveal even that much, but he trusted Colin without fail. Still, considering that his sister was wed to Montgomerie, he didn't wish to put his best friend in the awkward position of knowing more than he should.

Colin's brows collided. "Verra well, Broc. But I've known you long enough to know that there is something you need from me. Dinna beat about the bush. What is it?"

This wasn't going at all as Broc had intended, but Colin was right. Out of respect, Broc came directly to the point. "What's the tale on the brother?" he asked him, eyeing the door to be sure no one entered the hall whilst they spoke.

For an instant, Colin didn't reply. His expression remained pensive. And then he began. "There are at least two witnesses who claim a *giant . . . fair-haired*"—his eyes narrowed as he regarded Broc more closely—"Scotsman"—obviously coming to the right conclusion, for Colin averted his eyes an instant and then returned his gaze to Broc to finish matter-of-factly, "attacked them."

Broc remained collected under Colin's careful scrutiny and even managed a smile. "Giant, eh?"

"Aye." His tone was sober. "They *claim* he accosted them without provocation, murdered two men, one of them being the woman's half-brother, and then took the girl and fled, his knife pressed at her throat."

Broc had little respect for liars and less for those too craven to defend their fellows. His tone was full of contempt when he spoke. "Two witnesses, you say?" He lifted a brow. "Two men against one?"

"Against a giant," Colin reminded him. "And he threatened to kill her if they followed."

"Giant, my arse!" Broc exploded. "Damned chicken-hearted bastards!"

"Aye," Colin agreed, and seemed suddenly thoughtful.

"If she had been my mistress, I would have plucked out the man's tongue," Broc told him. He never would have chanced to have his knife at her throat in the first place! That's idiocy!"

Anger surged through him.

He twined his fingers together between his knees and stared down at the floor, trying to compose himself. Though he had the most over-whelming urge to defend himself, to tell Colin why he had done what he'd done, it was in no one's best interest for him to confess—not Colin's, not Seana's, not his own, and most as-suredly not Elizabet's.

What the hell was he going to do?

At the instant, he felt the weight of his decep-tion bearing down upon him. It was nearly as cumbrous as his obligation to Elizabet.

He shook his head, clenching his jaw in tor-ment.

Never in his life had he found himself so torn. The lines had always been clearly drawn for him—right was right, wrong was wrong, and his loyalty lay solely with his clan. This time, he couldn't even see the forest for the trees. No mat-ter what choice he made, someone was bound to suffer. God's holy truth, if he could have sacri-ficed himself and no other, he would have done so without hesitation.

But that wasn't the case.

If he turned himself in, he would place Eliza-bet in danger. After all, who would protect her and who would believe him? Certainly not Piers against the word of two witnesses. Not even Eli-zabet, for he had lied to her about her brother. If he revealed himself to Colin, then Colin would be forced to betray either his sister or his best friend. If he swore Seana to secrecy, he would be asking her to break faith with her husband. If he told Iain, he would oblige Iain to side with him against every other clan in the region—and Iain would do so, but Broc couldn't allow it.

No matter how he looked at it, he felt himself completely alone. And the only thing he knew of a certain was that he would never forgive himself if he allowed harm to come to Elizabet.

She trusted him . . . as Colin did . . . as Iain did.

Colin's tone was grave when he spoke. "Is there aught you wish to share with me, Broc?"

Broc shook his head, his gut twisting. He couldn't even look Colin in the eyes. "I just need time," he said, and the simple statement said far more than Broc should have provided.

Silence fell between them—a long silence that seemed impenetrable. Colin seemed to understand precisely what Broc could not say. When Broc peered again into his friend's eyes, they were sullen and distressed.

Seana came into the room just then, bearing a tray with beverages for the three of them. Along with the ale, she brought bread and cheese to snack on. With a heartwarming smile for her husband and another for Broc, she placed the tray on the table between them. Neither of them responded, with the mood between them as morose at it was.

She placed her hands upon her hips. "By Jacob's stone!" she declared. "The two of you look as though you've been sentenced to death! What in heaven could be so wrong?"

She looked from one to the other, waiting for an explanation.

"Broc isn't staying," Colin told her, rising abruptly from his seat at the table. "He merely came to wish us well."

Seana blinked in surprise. "But he only just arrived, Colin!"

Broc stood to go. He understood what Colin was telling him without having to hear it spoken. Years of friendship had given them a like mind. He didn't want Seana involved.

He and Colin shared a glance, and then Colin began to gather the bread and cheese from the tray. While Seana wasn't watching, he set the victuals within a napkin and wrapped it neatly, then came around the table to stand beside his wife.

" 'Tis late, Seana," Broc explained. "I just hadn't had the opportunity to speak to you after the wedding and wanted to wish you well together."

Seana smiled, but he could tell she didn't quite believe him, because she cast her husband a puzzled glance. She turned again to Broc. "I have much to thank you for, Broc. If it weren't for you, I'd never have found Colin."

Broc stepped forward to embrace her hastily. "Ye give me far too much credit, lass." He bent to place a chaste kiss high on her cheek. "Both of you always knew where the other was. You simply had to rediscover each other again, and you did that all by yourselves."

Seana tilted him a warm look. "Well, I thank you even so. Oh, Broc, you cannot imagine how much your friendship has always meant to me."

Broc winked at her. He did understand, far more than she realized, from the first instant when she'd looked up at him so reverently after he'd dried her tears as a child. Every day thereafter that she'd looked at him, he'd spied the gratitude in her eyes. And it was gratitude that had nearly convinced her she should become his wife. He saw all that and more in her sweet face, and he hadn't ever acknowledged her affection, because he hadn't wished her to feel she owed him anything at all. It took more than gratitude to make a good match, and he'd wanted more for Seana than to have her spend her entire life trying to repay him for a simple kindness. He had done no more than soothe a little girl's hurt feelings.

"And yours to me," he told her, tears stinging his eyes. He didn't know why, but the moment touched him more than he could say. He turned

then to Colin, quashing his unruly emotions.
God's teeth, he felt like a weepy wench at the
instant. "I'm sorry," he offered.

"For what?" Seana asked him, obviously confused by their fragmented discourse.

"For nothing," Colin replied at once, and then
to Broc he added, "We've known each other far
too long, my friend."

Broc placed his hands upon his hips, preparing
to take his leave. "Aye, that we have."

Seana watched them more curiously yet, saying nothing. Broc was keenly aware of her regard. She was smart, he knew, and he didn't
want her to ascertain what they were speaking
of. Still he had to ask, "Have you returned to the
hut, Seana?" He tried to sound casual.

"Nay," she answered, and sighed. "I've not. It
brings back too many memories as yet."

Broc nodded, understanding. Relief washed
through him. "I know what you mean, lass. Mayhap 'tis a good thing for you to stay away from
there for a while." He leveled a look at Colin,
knowing his friend would understand what he
was trying to say.

Seana's brows knit. "Mayhap so." She lifted
her chin as she turned to regard her husband
with narrowed eyes.

Colin slid an arm around her shoulders. "She
has no reason to return there at all."

Seana said nothing, merely reached up to

grasp her husband's hand, which dangled from her shoulder, and studied them both.

Broc nodded then and turned to go. "I hope to see the two of you verra soon."

"And I you," Colin replied.

Seana's tone was full of concern. "Be careful, Broc," she said, reaching out to grasp him by the arm.

He turned and winked at her. "I'm a big boy, lass. Dinna ye fret over me."

"Oh, Broc," Colin interjected then.

Broc tossed his chin up in reply.

"We'll be searching again tomorrow if you wish to join us."

For an instant, Broc was flustered by the suggestion. He was momentarily unsure whether Colin truly had understood the point of their discourse. "I may," he relented, but eyed his friend thoughtfully.

Colin held his gaze. "I believe they intend to use her dog tomorrow."

Broc knit his brows. "Her dog?"

Colin leveled him a significant look. "Aye, someone suggested mayhap the dog's nose would find her mistress sooner than our eyes."

Broc thought about that bit of information. "It makes quite a lot of sense," he said with a nod of comprehension. "Whoever suggested that is a wily bastard."

Colin nodded soberly. "I suggested it."

Broc smiled at him. "Figures."

Colin smiled back. "We'll be heading out about noon, I think . . . if you should care to join us."

All the while, Seana watched them, her expression growing more curious yet. Broc determined it was best to leave before they inadvertently gave something away. As it was, he had involved Colin far more than he'd intended to, far more than his conscience allowed. Guilt pricked at him.

Broc turned to go, and Colin followed him out, leaving Seana staring pensively after them.

"I owe you one," Colin murmured at Broc's back.

"You owe me nought," Broc assured him, without turning. They walked out the door.

"Aye, but I do," Colin argued, once they were outside. And then he added, "You saved my life once, Broc."

"I did no less than any friend would have done."

Colin nodded. "I have no notion what has happened to you, but I do know you, my friend, and I know you better than to think you would attack some innocent girl."

Broc's shoulders tensed. "I would never do so."

"I realize that," Colin acknowledged. "But I

canna promise you anything more than a little time."

Broc halted abruptly and turned to face him, his gut churning. "I didna ask ye for aught, Colin."

Colin smacked him on the arm. "You dinna have to." He handed Broc the cloth filled with food. "Dinna say anything more. The less I know, the better. Just go."

"Thank you, Colin."

"I know you would do the same for me" was all Colin said.

Broc turned one last time to go. "Without question."

"Oh, and by the by," Colin added. Broc cast him a glance but kept walking. "I know where you can find a lonely hound tonight." Broc turned to face him but kept walking—backward, toward the woods. He clutched the food for Elizabet tightly in his hand, lest it spill. "Montgomerie's stables," Colin disclosed. "That is . . . should you find yourself lonely for Merry."

Broc swallowed his response, so great were his emotions. He couldn't speak even to thank Colin. No man had ever been blessed with truer friends—and he repaid them all by endangering them by his duplicity.

Without a word, he turned again and bounded into the woods.

Chapter 16

"What was that about?" Seana asked her husband when he came into the hall, slamming the door behind him.

He went to her and placed his arm about her shoulders, his jaw taut as he coaxed her toward the staircase. "'Tis nought. Dinna worry about it, Seana."

"That wasna like him at all," she remarked, hoping he would elaborate. But she knew Colin well enough to know he wouldn't reveal whatever Broc had come to tell him. She respected his faithfulness but was hurt he wouldn't share with her.

They reached the stairs. "I'm weary," was all he said, stepping back, urging her to go before him.

Seana lifted her skirts and climbed the stairs. "'Tis been a long day, indeed!"

"Aye," he agreed, "and tomorrow should prove just as tiresome."

She reached the top of the stairs to find her brother-in-law's wife standing there, taper in hand. "I heard voices," Alison said, "and Leith is fast asleep. I didn't wish to wake him."

"It was only Broc," Colin reassured her, "come to find out about the search efforts."

"I do hope they find that poor girl soon!" Alison declared.

"As do I," Colin replied, patting her awkwardly on the shoulder. "Go back to sleep, Alison. All is well."

Alison turned a warm smile upon Seana. "Welcome home," she said with genuine enthusiasm, at least as much as could be expected so late in the eve.

Seana reached out to embrace her, taking care with the candle flame, grateful for the warm reception. "Thank you, dear Alison."

"It will be my pleasure to share this home with you. Please dinna hesitate to treat it as your own," Alison said with feeling, and Colin squeezed her shoulder slightly in response.

"I appreciate that, Alison," Seana replied.

Alison lingered in the hallway, looking warily up at Colin, and Seana understood. There was more to be said for their ears alone. Turning to

Colin, Seana whispered, "I'll be right in, my love."

Colin didn't argue. He nodded, evidently having far too much on his mind. He bent to kiss her upon the cheek and went into their room, closing the door to give them privacy.

Alison smiled shyly. "Sometimes I feel he still hates me," she said very softly.

It was no secret to any that Alison had once adored Colin and that he had rebuffed her. Considering that she and Alison now shared a house, as they were wed to brothers, Seana had worried that their relationship might be tense, but as she stood there looking at Alison's sweet face, she knew she had worried for nought. There was something about Alison that made one want to place one's arms about her shoulders and protect her from the world. Leith, Colin's elder brother and laird, had done that very thing, and everyone had speculated that their marriage had been born of pity. Seana knew better. Though she had never been close with Alison, she was wholly aware of the kind heart the woman possessed. Leith was a fortunate man. If Colin was uncomfortable in Alison's presence, then Seana understood better than any the reason why. He had once recoiled from Seana in the very same manner he recoiled from Alison, but Seana had nearly outgrown her disfigurement, and Alison had not. She resolved somehow to find a way to make Colin look beyond Alison's crossed eyes.

"He doesn't hate you," Seana told her, reaching out admiringly to caress the length of her shiny hair. She decided honesty was the best course between them. "He is just a clod when it comes to other people's imperfections."

Alison gasped in surprise and laughed nervously, casting a wary glance at the door.

It was also no secret to anyone that Seana had once had a frail limb and that Colin had been repulsed by the weakness. Seana winked at Alison, indicating her bad leg with a wave of her hand. "But as you can see, there is hope for him yet."

Placing a hand over her mouth, Alison giggled quietly.

"We'll get him past it somehow," Seana assured her new friend.

"I do hope so!" Alison declared. "It would be so wonderful to be one big happy family together."

"It truly would be." The very thought of it filled Seana with joy. Growing up, she had never had anyone but her father. And now, suddenly, she had a best friend in Meghan and a sister in Alison. And Colin . . .

She glanced longingly at the door.

He made her happier than anyone ever could.

"I shall see you on the morrow," Seana promised her.

Alison nodded. "Oh, yes!"

"Sweet dreams, then."

"Good night," Alison said, and turned to walk away.

Turning to her bedroom door, Seana paused an instant to say a little prayer of thanks and then pushed the door open to find her husband standing at the window, staring out.

"This *is* your home," he assured her, mistaking Alison's meaning.

She walked up to him and put her arms about him, embracing him lovingly as she reached up on tiptoes to kiss his lips. "I know," she assured him. "Alison is wonderful, and I know I shall love her as though she were my own sister."

"Aye, but rest assured this place is just as much yours as it is—"

She lifted a finger to his lips. "Hush, now," she demanded. "Why don't we test our new bed before anyone else chances to knock on our door?"

She didn't have to ask again.

With a quirk of his brow, he lifted her into his arms, and carried her to bed.

Elizabet sat at the little table, her face close to the candle flame, trying to finish the last stitches of the tunic she was sewing.

She had worked all day on the garment, fashioning it from the soft, fine cloth of her undertunic. She'd thought, at first, to cook for him, using the supplies he'd brought her, but they were depleted now, and she'd despaired of finding a suitable gift to show her appreciation for all he'd done for her. But then she'd recalled the needle and thread that she always carried in the hem of her dress to stitch her back into her gown after it had been laundered, and she'd set to work trying to fashion a tunic he would be proud to wear.

At this moment she wore only the velvety surcoat, which had a slightly more revealing neckline, but it couldn't be helped. She was warm enough, and she was thoroughly pleased with her handiwork. In truth, she had seen no finer garment on King Henry himself. Broc would look splendid in it.

Blinking with exhaustion, she sewed the last stitch and snipped the thread with her teeth, setting the needle aside. Later, she would return it to her hem. At the moment, she was far too weary even to move. She pushed the candle away from her and held up the tunic to inspect it, pleased with the finished product. She hoped it would fit him—he was so large a man!

He was beautiful, she thought wistfully.

God's truth, she almost dreaded Piers' return, because it would mean she could no longer remain here with Broc. The little hovel no longer seemed such a terrible place, and the thought of leaving it made her somehow sad. She almost regretted asking him to bring John to her. Once her brother realized where she was, it wouldn't be so simple a task to convince him she should remain with Broc at least until they revealed Tomas for the murdering thief he was.

Her brother would protest for propriety's sake. She knew it wouldn't look good to a prospective husband. This could sully her reputation beyond repair. But she couldn't consider that right now.

She yawned, then folded the cloth, setting it down on the table. And then she laid her head down upon her arms and closed her eyes.

Broc would take care of everything, she was certain. She felt safe in his care. John would surely understand ... why she must remain ... with Broc.

She reached out sleepily to lay her hand upon the soft tunic and fell asleep trying to imagine Broc's face when she presented it to him.

He had to get rid of the dog before morning.

Tomas sat listening to the conversation at table, trying not to roll his eyes at the elaborate show of affection between Montgomerie and his wife. The woman was no more than a Highland bitch, and he treated her as though she were the Queen of England herself. He had significant doubts about Piers' loyalties. The way he pandered to his wife and her kinsmen, he was behaving more like a backwoods Scotsman than a servitor of the Crown. He'd be damned if he'd hand over Elizabet's purse so that Piers could squander it on his doting wife.

By God, he deserved the monies! Meager as the sum was, he sure as hell hadn't bothered to kill two men only to lose it now. His sister would surely provide for him, but he didn't particularly care for the notion of having to beg for every coin he received from her. Elizabet's inheritance would see him through until Margaret's husband favored them with his passing.

He damned well didn't want the wench to be found. No one but he, John and Elizabet had been aware of the purse John carried, and neither did anyone else realize there was a letter intended for Piers. Even if he wished to let it go now, he couldn't. Elizabet would reveal far more than he could allow.

Later, when everyone had gone to bed, he would rid himself of the hound.

"Tomas?" his hostess inquired, turning him from his reverie. Until now, they had rudely excluded him from their conversation, discussing matters that hardly interested him.

The entire table now turned to him. Like her husband, the men seemed to hang on Meghan's every word. "Aren't you at all hungry?" she asked him and tilted her pretty head.

For sheep's gut?

Tomas lifted his brows as he glanced down at

the food, trying not to show his revulsion against the mess on his plate. He took a sip of his ale before replying. "I find myself weary, that is all, my lady."

" 'Tis understandable," she so graciously conceded. "It has been a wearisome day for all."

For an instant, he thought she might dismiss him from her table as one would an unmannerly child. It left him with a sour feeling in his belly, and he suddenly no longer cared for their company—not even for the ale. As soon as he had taken care of a few unfinished details, he intended to be away from this place once and for all.

He rose from the table abruptly, raking his chair back indecorously. "If you will be so kind as to excuse me," he said, taking his leave. "I believe I shall retire for the night."

"Pleasant dreams," Meghan said with a smile.

Bitch. He could see the relief flare in her expressive eyes.

"We shall see you bright and early on the morrow," Piers charged him.

Arrogant bastard.

Tomas could hardly wait for the day when he could stop taking orders from pompous arses.

He bowed slightly with barely restrained anger, clinging to future promise to temper his outrage. "Until tomorrow, then," he said and left them, feeling acutely their beady eyes on his back.

The sooner he was gone from here, the better.

He wished that damned bastard Scotsman who had taken Elizabet would put her in her place, rape her unruly little arse, and then slit her throat and leave her body for them to find.

Then he could leave in peace.

Chapter 17

Having come directly from Colin's home to Montgomerie's, Broc watched from the shelter of the small, partially constructed chapel, waiting for the manor to still.

The chapel was likely a donation to Gavin's ministry, and it was a generous gesture on Meghan's part, though Broc knew without doubt that Colin would curse her for it. Neither Leith nor Colin would encourage their youngest brother's sermonizing, and unless Piers had a taste for self-torture—and Broc didn't think so—he wouldn't have offered, either.

The chapel was nearly completed. It lacked glass in the windows and a door, but the interior had been scrubbed clean and prepared for John's funeral. His body lay resting upon a bier behind the altar. He would have been buried already, but Broc was certain that out of respect for Elizabet they were hoping to find her in time to lay him properly to rest.

But they wouldn't wait much longer.

Guilt pricked at him, though he resolutely set it aside, focusing on the task at hand.

Donning a robe he found near the altar, he left the chapel and made his way to the stables. It was Gavin's robe, he decided, as he adjusted its length over his limbs. Gavin was far shorter than he was, and the gown fell only to midcalf. Still, its hood covered his face well enough, and that was all that he was concerned with at the moment.

He didn't wish to find himself face to face with Tomas or either of the other two lackeys. As yet, no one seemed to know it was Broc they were looking for—save mayhap Colin—but he was certain they would recognize him if they spied him again.

Casting one last glance over his shoulder at the little building, he admired its modest architecture and wondered what Elizabet would look like on her wedding day with her hair let down and a circlet of flowers on her head.

It was obvious that she was accustomed to finer things than Broc was possessed of. Still, he liked to think he could make her happy if he tried—if she would have him.

It was the first time in his life that he'd ever

considered matrimony an option for himself, and
he didn't like what he saw. He had nothing to
his name, no manor, no clan of his own, no
wealth. All he had was his heart and his body
and a small house with scarce a single luxury to
his name—a bed, a chair, a table, and a blanket.
Everything he'd ever earned he'd given to others, for his needs were simple and few. He found
himself wanting.

God's truth, what would a woman like that
desire of a man like him?

She was beautiful and saucy and intelligent—
and he wondered what she was doing right now.
He worried that she would wander away, worried that someone would catch him and that she
would be alone without anyone to help her. If
he was afeared to be found out, it wasn't for himself. It was for her. Broc was convinced, after her
revelations to him, that it was Tomas who
wanted her dead. What he didn't know was
whether Tomas was acting alone or whether he
had the aid of the other two men.

He couldn't allow himself to be caught. And
he damned well couldn't allow that hound to remain in their possession. Colin's suggestion had
been ingenious, and Broc had little doubt the animal could find its mistress, given the opportunity.

He wasn't going to give it the opportunity.

Elizabet would be more than pleased to see her

four-legged friend again. He just needed to steal the animal from the stables without anyone catching him—a task that was easier said than done.

He heard voices inside the stables. Keeping to the shadows, he searched within, trying to find the bearers. Whispers, low and intimate, reached his ears, but he couldn't see the persons speaking. There was a giggle, then—very feminine and a lower, huskier response—lovers?

They must have placed a guard, but Broc didn't see him. Mayhap he had an affectionate visitor and they were ensconced in one of the stalls? In any case, it wasn't any of his affair. All he cared about was the dog. Slipping within, he walked lightly, trying not to alert the stable's other occupants.

The voices grew louder the further he went, and he determined they were within the last stall, where a single lantern hung high upon a post. Ignoring their lovers' banter, he checked each stall, moving as swiftly as he was able without disturbing them.

As Colin promised, he found the dog tied to a stake within the third stall he checked. On either side of him, the steeds stamped their hooves and snorted uneasily. Wincing at their protests, he opened the stall, startling the sleeping dog to its feet.

Broc flung back his hood at once, letting the

animal see him. Its ears flew back, as though in
startle, but it remained quiet, watching him. Broc
thought mayhap it recognized him, and his as-
sumption proved correct. He extended his hand,
kneeling, and the dog took a step toward him,
sniffing his palm. He praised the mongrel silently, reaching out to pat its neck. The animal
relaxed, shuddering, as Broc stroked it. It began
to sniff his legs, finding the napkin he'd secured
beneath his belt, and then rosing Broc's clothes,
likely sensing its mistress. It whined softly, peering up at him, cocking its head as though in
question.

Broc stilled, but the animal only whined
louder. He held his breath, hoping the lovers
hadn't heard.

"Damned mongrel!" the man exclaimed. Broc
stifled a groan. "I should go check on him,
Emma."

"Nayyy," Emma wailed in protest. She must
have held him fast, because Broc didn't hear the
lad rise to his feet.

"I fed the stupid animal already," her lover
reasoned. "I cannot imagine what it could want."

" 'Tis a silly mutt," Emma declared, her voice
turning coy, "and if you leave me like this, I'm
going to whine louder than he does!"

Her lover laughed, obviously amused by her
pouting. "I do like it when you whimper," he
assured her.

Broc rolled his eyes.

The two of them giggled together and evidently returned to their pleasures, because Broc heard no one approach. He thought he heard them smacking their lips together and tried not to think about Elizabet—what it would be like to kiss her again. She had the softest-looking lips, perfectly formed.

Saucy wench.

When no footsteps became apparent after another moment, Broc breathed a sigh of relief and replaced the hood over his head, preparing to go. He untied the rope from the stake with one hand and petted the animal with the other.

Now to get the bloody beast out of the stables. He cracked open the door and peered out, then pushed it open when he was certain the way was clear. He led the dog out by the rope, closing the stall door carefully behind him, and then hurried outside. Once in the courtyard, he made his way to the meadow, grateful for the near moonless night. It was at least two furlongs before he would reach the forest, and he hurried toward it, longing for its sanctuary, murmuring praise to the animal once he was far enough away for no one to hear him. He called it by its name, and it followed happily.

It wasn't until he was near the forest's edge that he heard bellows. He peered over his shoulder, expecting to find himself being pursued, and froze where he stood.

The stable had suddenly burst into flames.

From the raging bonfire bounded a squealing, bucking stallion, its mane afire. The sight of it, even at the distance, brought Broc to his knees.

He couldn't tell whether the shouts came from those he'd left within or from those who were hurrying toward the growing inferno. His gut twisted with indecision. He prayed the couple he'd left within would make it out of the flames and was torn between wanting to go back and help them and wanting to flee the scene before he was discovered. He tried to recall whether he had inadvertently caused the fire and was absolutely certain he had not. There had been no lights within the stable, no flames, except the one at the far end of the aisle where the lovers lay. Surely they had started the fire themselves and had fled to safety, though his heart ached for the animals left inside.

The shouts intensified as the fire grew fiercer. Silhouettes scurried about in chaos.

Taking the leash in hand, Broc took one last look at the melee and ducked into the woods, pulling the dog behind him. He ran as fast as the animal could go without dragging it in his wake. He ran, keeping Elizabet in mind. Because if he didn't, if he for one instant forgot what was at stake, he would turn around and go back.

*   *   *

"I saw the arrow fly," Baldwin informed Piers. "With my own eyes!"

Piers knew Baldwin wouldn't lie. The man had been with him far too long.

Ordering his wife to remain inside, he turned and slammed open the doors, bursting into the night's chaos.

Who the hell had cause to burn his stables? And someone had, there was no mistaking it. A burning arrow shot into the air was certainly no accident!

"Who was left within?" Piers snapped at Baldwin.

"No one, Piers! No one, though young David and his wench were inside when it happened. The girl made it out fine. David remained to open the stalls and suffered severe burns because of it, but he's out, at least, albeit in pain."

Piers scowled. "Brave lad."

"Aye, we owe him our gratitude."

"I'll see he is rewarded for his efforts."

Baldwin nodded. "He saved at least five mounts. Two were not so fortunate . . ." He hesitated. "Yours being one of them."

An explosion of curses erupted from Piers' tongue. "By God's teeth, if I discover the culprit, I swear I will cut off his arms and his legs and then hang him from the nearest tree to feed the vultures!"

Baldwin winced.

Piers came to a halt before the stable and stood, arms akimbo, glaring at the burning building. His men scurried about, trying in vain to put out the flames. They weren't equipped to battle fires. The well was too far, the water supply insufficient. Their best course was to let it extinguish itself.

Thank God the stables had been constructed apart from the manor house and far from the forest. As it was, he was in danger of losing the barracks behind it, but thankfully no more than that. He'd fully intended to build a new one in time, but he damned well couldn't afford to do so at the moment. And yet there was no help for it. He couldn't do without housing for his men. The horses would have to be put out in the field, and the fences would have to be secured, but the weather was mild as yet, and he wasn't so concerned about the beasts.

God damn whoever was responsible!

"Holy Christ!" a voice shouted from a distance. "What the hell happened here?"

It was Tomas. His arrival couldn't have been more ill timed.

Or more perfect, as the case might be.

Piers cast him a rancorous glance, wondering where the hell he had been riding so late.

"I thought you were going to retire for the night," he said to the man with barely restrained animosity. There was something nefarious about his guest, something he had sensed from the first instant their eyes had met. If there hadn't been two bloody witnesses to corroborate his story, Piers might have called him a liar to his face.

"I wasn't tired, so I thought to take another look about for Elizabet," he said.

"How convenient," Piers replied acidly, clenching his teeth. He formed a fist without realizing it and released it, trying to remain calm. He silently urged the man to keep his distance, because he was about to rip his tongue from his throat.

"Damned convenient if ye ask me," Baldwin said low beside him.

Tomas seemed to ignore the barb. "I feel so responsible," he said with feigned sorrow, as he dismounted beside them. "Her father placed her in my care. I feel as though I've failed him."

Piers was still glaring at him. The man turned to face the burning stables, averting his gaze. "What happened?" he asked again. "Someone drop a lantern into the hay? Careless buggers!" He spat upon the ground.

"Nay," Piers corrected him, somehow certain Tomas knew far more about the blaze than he was willing to admit. "Someone torched it."

Tomas turned to face Piers, his expression marked with the same lack of emotion he had displayed in the case of John's death.

No conscience.

No concern.

Nought but an empty expression.

"So you were worried about Elizabet?" Piers asked him.

God damned liar!

"Aye," Tomas replied, and turned again to stare at the rising flames. "What about the dog?" he asked without turning again to regard Piers. His voice was toneless.

Piers merely stared at the man, a seed of suspicion beginning to take root.

Baldwin burst forth with a string of blasphemies. "The damned dog!" he said, swiping at the air in anger. "We forgot about that damned dog!"

"What a pity," Tomas replied and continued to stare into the flames.

Piers blinked at his response.

He peered back in the direction the man had come from, trying to gauge the distance an arrow could fly. He turned then to Baldwin and asked him, "From which direction did the arrow come?"

Baldwin was still cursing over the loss of the dog. "That way," he said, indicating the direction Tomas had ridden from with a nod of his head.

"I see," Piers said, flicking Tomas another glance. The man was still staring into the flames, but Piers was well aware Tomas's attention was directed at him.

He was responsible, and Piers was going to prove it.

Without another word, he spun on his heel and left Baldwin to deal with the fire, because if he had to remain in Tomas's presence even an instant longer, he was going to seize the man by the throat and rip out his lying, conniving tongue!

Chapter 18

Broc was out of breath when he reached the hut.

Guilt tore at him for leaving the scene of the fire. The images and sounds tormented him. Screams and shouts filled his senses. Roaring flames stung his eyes.

Those were his friends he'd abandoned back there. He should have pitched in to help put out that fire.

He should have but he hadn't dared.

He pushed the door to the hut open. "Elizabet?" he called out. The room was dark save for the light of a single taper that sat on the table. She was asleep, her head resting upon the table, her hair flowing down her back like a river of copper silk. Smiling at the sight of her, for he could scarce help himself, he knelt to untie

Harpy's leash. The dog wagged its tail anxiously, peering up at him in what Broc sensed to be appreciation. He patted the animal affectionately, grateful he had gotten to the stable before the fire.

He still could not fathom how the fire had started. The lantern had been placed far too high for careless lovers to have tipped it. It was possible the lantern had simply dropped, but the handle had appeared secure enough.

He was reluctant to let Harpy go to her. God's truth, he'd never seen a more beautiful sight. In sleep she looked like an angel, her skin translucent in the light of the flame. He studied her while he could, taking pleasure in the moment. Her pert little nose was delicate and refined, her cheeks high and gently chiseled. Her brows were dark and sharply arched. Her look was exotic and lovely. More lovely than anything he'd ever seen in his life.

And that hair—how he would have loved to tangle his fingers in that glorious hair!

With a sigh and a last rub behind the animal's ears, he let the dog go. Harpy bounded at once toward Elizabet, tail wagging happily. Broc couldn't suppress his laughter as Elizabet woke in alarm. His shoulders shook with mirth.

"Ack!" she exclaimed, and nearly tumbled from the chair, disoriented by sleep. She stumbled to her feet. It took her a befuddled moment to realize what had awakened her.

"My God!" she exclaimed when she realized it was her dog, and she threw out her arms in welcome. "Harpy!"

Broc chuckled, momentarily distracted from the evening's hideousness. How could he not smile when watching the two of them together? Away flew the haughty maiden; on her knees went a little girl filled with glee over the return of her pet. She hugged the animal fiercely, letting it lap her on the forehead. She giggled with joy and buried her face against its fine coat, trying to avoid the animated tongue.

Broc sat transfixed, feeling an overwhelming sense of closeness to her. He watched her, his heart feeling strangely elevated by the sight of them together.

Her dress seemed different somehow, the color faded beneath a layer of dust. Her hair was loose and far messier than he'd ever seen it—och, but it was beautiful. Its color was brilliant even in the shadows of the room. Burnished with streaks of copper, it gleamed wherever the candle's light touched it. Her smile was radiant, illuminating the room more brilliantly than even a torch could have done.

God help him. He fell in love with her in that instant.

"You found her!" she said, peering up at last.

Broc swallowed his words, speechless for a moment. He nodded.

She turned that smile upon him, and his knees threatened to pitch him over. "Where was she?"

"They tied her to a post in Montgomerie's barn."

Her tone was excited now. "So you saw my brother!"

God's truth, he didn't want to lie, but he felt compelled to. He forced a nod, feeling lower than he'd ever felt in all his life. He told himself it wasn't entirely a lie. After all, he *had* seen John's body.

"What did he say?"

He couldn't take the lie quite that far.

He shook his head. "I know I promised, but I didna speak to him." He tempered the lie with a bit of truth. "There was a fire. 'Twas all I could do to take the dog and go."

"A fire?"

"Aye." He averted his gaze for an instant to recover his composure. "It appears someone burned down the stables," he told her, his gut twisting with self-disgust.

"Piers will be furious!" she said.

Broc nodded agreement. "I'm certain." He tried to recall if anyone had had opportunity to spy him. The circumstances were building against him. Everything he had worked for, everything he had achieved, the trust he had built, the friends he had earned, all of it was crumbling before his eyes. In the span of just a few days, everything seemed suddenly grimmer than hell.

And on top of everything else, he loved a woman he couldn't have.

"What did you do while I was gone?" he asked, feeling suddenly fatigued.

She stroked her dog, smiling sweetly at him. "I kept my promise."

"Promise?"

Her smile curved into a sheepish grin. "I stayed out of trouble, of course."

He was glad one of them had, at least.

What he wouldn't have given for her to hold him with that same affection she was lavishing upon her dog.

"Lucky dog," he said low.

She lifted her head. "What did you say?"

He smiled back at her. "I said Harpy's a good dog."

Elizabet was certain he hadn't said any such thing. She tilted him a curious look, wondering if she should trust her ears. God forgive her, but she was almost relieved he hadn't spoken to John yet.

The truth was . . . she didn't want to leave him. She averted her gaze, afeared he would read her thoughts. "So," she asked, trying to determine how much time was left, "did you learn when Piers would be returning?"

"Soon," he assured her.

There was something about his demeanor when he spoke of John and Piers that disturbed her, but she couldn't quite place her finger on what it was. Still, she trusted him, and knew he would do the right thing. There was something virtuous about him—not pious but pure. Whenever she peered into his eyes, she thought she knew what angels looked like. But those eyes seemed troubled tonight, and she hoped he wasn't regretting helping her.

"Is aught wrong?"

He shook his head. "Nay, lass, I'm only weary, that's all."

Their gazes held, locked, his blue eyes regarding her with an expression that quickened her breath.

"I did something else while you were gone," she disclosed, giving him a coy smile. She stood and walked over to the table.

He watched her curiously.

She lifted up the square of neatly folded bright red cloth and held it in her hands. " 'Tis a gift," she told him. "For you."

His bewilderment was apparent in his eyes. "For me?"

Elizabet smiled. "Aye." She walked forward, handing him the garment.

He accepted it, albeit a bit uncertainly. He didn't even look at it for the longest time, merely stared at her, his arms outstretched with the garment in hand.

She pushed it toward him, afeared he would return it to her. "Aren't you going to try it on?"

He swallowed. Elizabet could see the knob in his throat bob. "No one has ever given me a gift before."

Elizabet arched a brow at him. "Try it on," she demanded.

He nodded, giving his attention for the first time to the tunic in his hands. He shook it out, examining it, clearly admiring her handiwork.

Elizabet warmed with pride.

He set it on the table to better inspect it and ran his fingers gently over the precise stitches. His gaze snapped up suddenly, as though only just realizing from whence the material had come.

"Och, lass, ye didna have to ruin your gown to make this tunic for me."

"I will surely be insulted if you think my gown ruined!" Her mother's despotic demeanor crept into her voice. "Put it on!"

He smiled then as he said, "Haughty wench!"

"I come by it honestly," she assured him and winked.

A strange smile came into his eyes suddenly as he regarded her.

Her heart began to beat a little faster at the expression on his face.

"So ye wish me to try it on, do ye?"

Elizabet nodded, even suspecting what he meant to do. She swallowed convulsively. God help her, she wanted to see how the tunic fitted his body, wanted to see how his muscles strained against the cloth, and she wanted that without apology.

She had never been disgusted by her mother's profession, but neither had she been fascinated by it. Never in her life had she been more beguiled by a man's body than she was by Broc's. Since the moment he'd sat before her in the chair with the blanket draped over him, completely unashamed, she hadn't been able to stop thinking of him.

He watched her as though trying to read her thoughts, and she straightened her shoulders, lifting her chin. "Go on, take it off," she challenged him. "I'm not some child who will squeal with mortification and cover my eyes."

Broc shook his head, assuring her, "I have never mistaken you for a child, lass."

He watched her expression, willing her to understand. God's truth, she had no idea what he was in danger of revealing.

Her mere presence tempted him beyond reason, and now she was asking him to undress and remove the one barrier that kept him civilized. Beneath his plaid, his body was rigid and throbbing.

He wanted her more than he'd ever wanted anyone or anything in his life.

Until now, denying his physical needs had been a simple enough endeavor, but what he wanted from her was far more than simple relief for his body. His soul cried out to possess her, his body longed to be touched by her. He wanted to be inside her—to pleasure her—to hear her whisper his name as he spilled his seed into her body. He wanted her to bear his babes, wanted to share his bed with her, wanted to bring her gifts and see her smile with joy, as she had moments before.

No one else could satisfy him.

But he wanted her willing. He wouldn't force her.

He would love her till his dying breath, but he wanted her to come to him of her own accord. He couldn't offer her a life of riches, but he could protect her and care for her.

He wasn't blessed with a smooth tongue, as Colin was. It wasn't his way. He said what he meant and meant what he said. "If ye wish to see me in this tunic, lass, ye will have to undress me yourself."

He issued the challenge without apology and held out the tunic for her to take.

He was a warm-blooded man, not some cold,

unfeeling stone, and he'd already used up what little restraint he possessed. If she removed from him his only defense against her, his clothing, he wasn't going to be held responsible for what happened after.

Her eyes widened slightly, but she said nothing to refuse him, merely stood there. When she didn't reach out to accept the tunic, he thought she might be offended, but then she dared to step forward. She took the tunic from his hands, nodding once, her expression apprehensive.

A shudder of anticipation passed through him.

Christ, he hoped she understood what she was getting into. If she touched him, if she peeled his feeble armor from his body, he wasn't going to walk away.

She reached out to touch his plaid, and he seized her wrist, holding it away from him. His loins tightened. "Are ye certain?"

Her hand felt so small in his grasp, soft and delicate. It was a testament to her birth. Though she claimed not to have been born to wealth, it was certain these hands had never seen a day's hard labor. His mother had toiled over the good earth for every morsel of food she had placed in her mouth and those of her husband and children.

It was just another reminder that Elizabet wasn't of his ilk.

"Aye," Elizabet said, and seemed to choke on her reply. "I wish to see you. . . .

A smile turned one corner of his mouth. He was certain she didn't mean it quite so directly.

Or mayhap she did.

It didn't matter.

Had she been the most brazen harlot on the face of the earth, it wouldn't have changed the way he felt about her. Nor would it have changed the way his body responded to the warmth of her skin—the elusive scent of her— the way she made him long to embrace her . . . protect her . . .

He pulled her closer, wanting nothing more than to kiss her in that instant.

Chapter 19

Elizabet's breath caught at the strength of his ardor.

He bent to kiss her.

She didn't resist, didn't want to.

Her heart beat faster as he took her into his arms, tangling his fingers in her hair. "You are so beautiful," he whispered. "So verra beautiful . . ."

She went limp in his embrace.

"I want you, Elizabet. . . ."

No one had ever said such a thing to her. The shock of hearing his husky plea left her momentarily dumb. She clung to him brazenly, her heart pounding ruthlessly against her breast.

And then he kissed her—and it was like nothing she'd ever imagined a man's lips would feel

241

like. They were soft and persistent . . . full of hunger. . . .

Sweet Mary, it was like nothing she'd ever dreamed of.

She had seen lovers embrace this way and then steal away to some secret place where no one could spy them. And she had secretly envied them, wondering what it must feel like to belong to someone else, to know that the arms that held her cherished her. She had watched men use and discard her mother so easily and sworn to God she would never fall prey to soft words whispered against her ear.

And here she was, willing to take whatever he would give her. And worse . . . Her heart wrenched with fear. Her legs trembled beneath her, threatening to make her sink at his feet.

"Broc," she pleaded, clinging to him desperately, but he only kissed her more insistently.

She was afraid to open her heart. Afraid to want. Afraid to hope. Men said whatever served them best until they used up what was inside and without another thought tossed away the shell that remained. Her mother had died alone, abandoned and empty. Only Elizabet had been at her side. Jesu, she would rather be alone if that was how she was meant to die. At least she would not suffer hope only to be aggrieved by its death.

"Och, lass," he murmured against her lips, his

mouth searing her. "I think I love you . . ."

Elizabet's heart jolted nearly out of her breast at the unexpected declaration.

"Nay!" she replied at once, turning her face from his fiery kisses. His lips singed her, his words burned deep into her heart. The possibility that he might not mean them daunted her more than she could have anticipated.

Her mother had left her alone, no matter that it hadn't been her choice to do so. Her father had sent her away with little more thought than he would have given to washing his hands. Piers was like to deny her, too. Why should this man want her when her own father did not?

"You cannot possibly love me!"

Every time she had ever dared to hope she might have a place to call her own, a family to embrace her, she was left disheartened.

When she tried to turn away, his hands cupped her face, forcing her gently to look into his eyes. "Aye, lass, I do," he swore. "Look at me!"

She could face his desire and match it with her own, but nay, she could not allow herself to hope!

"I love you, Elizabet."

Her father had once said that to her mother, as well, but it hadn't meant he'd wanted her to share his life. He'd abandoned them both, returning to his wife and the children she'd borne him.

She didn't want to hear that he loved her!

"How can you say such a thing to me?" she asked him, her tone accusatory.

He met her anger with compassion, smiling down at her, daring to look as though he meant every word he spoke. Despite her resolve not to feel it, a tiny ember of hope flared up within her.

"How can you say that?" she begged to know.

He held her close, looking into her eyes, as he said with feeling, "Because I never had purpose to my life until I met you, Elizabet."

She parted her lips to speak, but he placed a finger to them, shushing her.

"And I know I love you because I've never missed anyone more than I miss you when I'm not with you."

Elizabet's heart flowered at his words. She wanted to believe him. God help her, she'd missed him too, thought about him every instant he wasn't with her. With every stitch she had sewn this afternoon, she'd yearned for his return.

"And I know because . . . I have never looked into anyone's eyes and felt as though I'd been struck in my belly!"

Her eyes stung with tears. She couldn't help it. His declaration made her choke on joyful laughter. Sweet as his words were, he made it sound as though love were a terrible curse.

He smiled at her. "Och, lass . . . I pledge ye my heart and ye answer me with laughter?"

Elizabet gasped aloud, afeared she had hurt his feelings. "Nay, oh, nay! I only—"

He hushed her with another kiss.

He was so handsome, his long golden hair like shining silk. "In truth I am not so skilled with words, my love. Alas, I am merely a poor Highland lad too stubborn to know when a lass is too gentle-born to have me."

Elizabet shook her head. " 'Tis God's truth that I am no more gentle born than you!"

"Ye dinna understand." He reverently touched her face with the callused pads of his fingers. "This face, unlike mine, has not weathered the harsh sunlight. It is silky, pale and perfect, bonny and sweet."

Elizabet blinked at his tender description of her.

His hand grasped hers then, turning them for their mutual inspection. "And these hands have never labored a day. They are smooth and delicate, made for finer things than bleach and wash."

But she could learn. She opened her mouth to assure him that she was no wilting flower, but he shushed her with another kiss on the lips. This time, his mouth opened slightly over hers, his tongue sliding out to lap her lower lip ever so gently. Elizabet's heart beat a little faster at the tenderness in his kiss.

Her head fell back, yearning for more, but he withdrew once again.

"I know I have no right to ask ye, Elizabet, but if ye will allow me to . . . I will care for ye always. No harm would ever come to ye, and no man but me would dare to touch you."

Was he asking her to wed with him?

The possibility left her dumb.

"As God is my witness, I will never fail you," he swore fervently. "And ye will live as best I can provide and die an old woman asleep in your bed."

It was the most unpoetic proposal she could ever have imagined, but something about the look in his eyes gave it the dreamy romanticism she had always dreamed a proposal of marriage would have.

A wistful smile crept into his eyes. "Can ye fancy yourself wed to a Scots barbarian like me?"

If she'd harbored any doubts about his intentions, he dismissed them at once with his self-deprecating question. Tears welled in her eyes. She shook her head to deny them. "You are not a barbarian, silly man!"

He gave her a playful wink. "Aye, but ye said so," he reminded her, and kissed her high upon the cheek, then unexpectedly lapped the teardrop from her face.

Elizabet's breath caught over the intimacy of the gesture.

"And I believe every word that comes from that beautiful mouth," he swore, as he bent to brush his lips over hers.

Elizabet could do nothing but cling to him wantonly.

She wanted his kisses, needed his embrace somehow more than anything she'd ever needed in her life.

He combed his fingers through her hair, his expression full of ardor. "I wish you would wear it this way always," he entreated.

Sweet Jesu, in that instant, she would have done anything he asked if only he continued to kiss her—talk to her that way—hold her as though he cherished her truly.

Could it be so?

Dare she hope?

Sometimes the most beautiful things came from the most hideous circumstances, her mother had once claimed. Until now, she hadn't begun to realize what her mother had meant.

He gazed at her adoringly, brushing her hair with his fingers, and she melted into his arms. "It shimmers by candlelight," he told her.

"Hush," she demanded, and like a wanton, she reached up on tiptoes, letting her head fall back in supplication. She didn't care. She wanted his kisses. "Kiss me again," she beseeched him.

She didn't have to ask him twice.

It didn't escape Broc that she hadn't answered his question as yet, but it didn't matter at the instant. Like a drunkard drawn to his drink, he bent to taste her once more, reveling in the sweet softness of her lips. If she would refuse his offer of marriage, so be it, but he wasn't strong enough to walk away from whatever she was willing to give him.

Before her, he was like a beggar with his hand outstretched. He wanted her heart but would settle for her body. He wanted her love but would settle for her passion. He wanted her forever but he would cherish the moment.

"Open your mouth for me, Elizabet."

He wanted inside.

She parted her lips, and his body shuddered in response. She had no notion what it was she was doing to him or how fevered he was becoming. She couldn't possibly know. Her hands gripped his shoulders in supplication, and he understood better than she what it was she yearned for. He wanted it, too. His body hardened fully.

It had been far too long.

He wanted her far too much.

Thirsting for the taste of her, he thrust his tongue between her lips, savoring the silky depths of her mouth. She moaned softly, and he deepened the kiss, embracing her covetously, lest she end the kiss too soon. The scent of her was driving him mad. The taste of her mouth left him intoxicated.

Without a word, he lifted her into his arms, never breaking the kiss, and carried her to the pallet in the corner of the room. He didn't want to give her the chance to refuse him, but he didn't want to ravage her, either. If she would deny him, so be it, but he felt a desperation to join with her unlike anything he'd ever felt in his life.

Tomorrow might be too late.

He didn't want to think about the consequences right now, nor the threat that hovered over them both. Nor did he want to think about what she would do when she discovered that her brother was dead. It mattered not that his death wasn't at Broc's hands. He was afeared she would blame him once she discovered the truth.

But he wasn't going to think about that at the moment. He wanted only to feel her from the inside. He wanted to bury himself deep within her.

He laid her gently down, kissing her still.

Elizabet cleaved to him, afraid he would leave her. Her hands went about his neck, holding him fast. She was drowning in his ardor but afeared to breathe, lest the moment be lost. Never had she felt so hungry for a man's embrace. It was as though his kiss had awakened some dormant yearning and if he dared to stop, she would be left unfulfilled.

Only after he pulled himself away from her, peering down into her face, did she become fully aware of where she lay. He hovered over her, watching her intently, his eyes glittering with some unnamed emotion.

Swallowing convulsively, her hand slid from his neck to his bare chest, her heart beating so fiercely that she thought it would burst. Like warm silk, his muscles danced beneath her palm. Reveling in the feel of his skin, her hand slid beneath the sash that fell across his chest only to discover a soft patch of hair that made her yearn to tangle her fingers within it.

He was a feast for her eyes . . . and hands . . . her senses . . .

He clasped his hand over hers and moved it to cover the sash. "I would have ye finish what you started," he whispered.

For an instant, she didn't understand what he meant, but then he squeezed her hand, forcing her to take a firm grasp of his dress.

Elizabet stared into his eyes, her heart hammering insistently now. She understood what he wanted from her, and she wanted to give it to him—she truly did. But she was afeared. And God's truth, she hadn't the first notion of how to remove the garment he was wrapped in. She tugged on it, then hesitated, and he smiled at her in approval.

"That's it, love." His hand moved down to his belt, and he began to unfasten it, watching her, the look in his eyes intense.

God, but his gaze alone left her quivering.

He unfastened the belt and tossed it aside. There seemed suddenly a purpose to his every look, his every move. And her body somehow understood, because even though he wasn't touching her, every nerve in her body became keenly aware of his proximity.

As she lay there, anticipating him, her breasts began to ache, and her body warmed.

"Do ye ken what I want, lass?"

Elizabet nodded jerkily, her body trembling slightly.

He hesitated and then asked, "Do ye want me to stop now?"

She shook her head, absolutely certain that was not what she wanted. Jesu, if he left her now, she thought she would die.

She wanted him to mean everything he said to her, wanted him to want her, wanted him to love her. Though she was afraid to say she loved him, too, some place deep down she knew she must. No man had ever reached past her defenses and made her feel the things he made her feel.

Never before had she been tempted this far.

Her fingers trembled as she gripped his sash,

but her heart pounded like a drumbeat in her ears.

She couldn't do it, didn't know how to undress him.

But she certainly knew how to undress herself. Taking a deep breath for courage, she let her hand fall from the sash to her bosom. Without the under-tunic beneath, all she needed to do was pull the surcoat aside and reveal herself to him.

That brazen gesture was sure to tell him all he needed to know. His gaze followed her hand down, and his expression fell with disappointment for the briefest instant until she caught hold of her dress. She clasped it firmly, her fingernails digging into the velvety garment until she could feel them like claws against her palm. He swallowed. She could see the knob in his throat rise, then fall, and she reveled in the power she seemed suddenly to have over him.

Her breasts arched toward him of their own accord, her body responding in some instinctive way. He never even blinked but seemed to be waiting eagerly to see what she would do. With a soft gasp, she drew the gown aside, watching his expression closely.

He sucked in a breath at what she revealed to him, and she smiled timidly. As though to compose himself, he closed his eyes and swallowed hard. When he opened them again, his face was flushed and his desire was writ plainly in his features. But he didn't move to touch her.

Emboldened by the look on his face, she dared to take her breast fully into her hand, and she began to caress it slowly while he watched, tempting him to touch her, pleading without words.

"Och, lass," he said, and it sounded vaguely like a protest. "Ye dinna have any notion what you are doing to me."

He growled softly then and reached out to cover her hand with his own, joining the erotic caress of her flesh. His touch further emboldened her, and she smiled up at him, moaning softly as their hands jointly stroked her body. He pushed her hand away suddenly, exposing her to his eyes once more.

"Beautiful," he whispered, and bent to touch his tongue to her nipple, tugging it gently into his mouth.

Elizabet gasped in pleasure, her hand falling helplessly at her side while he suckled at her bosom. His expression alone sent her senses reeling. His face, shadowed on one side and lit on the other by golden light, was more beautiful in that moment than she could have ever imagined. No artist could have painted the intensity of that expression. No brush could have revealed the glimmer in his hair. No words could have expressed the passion depicted upon his face. One hand cupped the side of her breast, scarce touching it, while he suckled with eyes closed, seeming to draw from her body his manna.

She could do nothing but watch . . . and cry out in pleasure.

Chapter 20

Broc had never wanted to please a woman more than he yearned to please Elizabet. He wanted to possess her body and soul. She was the most beautiful thing ever to come into his life, and he didn't want to think of what it would be like returning to a life without her.

If only for tonight, he wanted to imagine she was his . . . would be his until he took his last breath.

He suckled her beautiful breasts, imagining his future bairns nourished there. He would die a happy man if he could merely hold her this close every night for the rest of his life. He would do anything to please her, never let harm come to her, cherish her always.

His heart had nearly burst through his ribs when she bared herself to him so artlessly and then arched her breasts seductively toward his hungering lips.

He divested himself of his dress while he suckled her, wanting to give her time to object. If she would deny him, he wanted to hear it now, before it was too late. He wanted her to know his desires, wanted her to see what she'd done to him—what she continued to do to him with the simple sound of her voice . . . a mere glance . . .

The scent of her skin was driving him mad. His body was hard, hungry.

He tore himself away from the feast she had offered, still ravenous with desire, and looked down at her flushed face. Her eyes were closed, her breasts arched upward, silently begging for more. Her nipple was dark and wet and shiny from his kisses, and his mouth was left wanting, with the taste of her sweet flesh lingering like ambrosia on his lips.

Christ, she was lovely.

When he was wholly divested, she opened her eyes and gasped audibly as her eyes fastened upon his erect shaft. For an instant, he thought she would cry out in fear, because her lips parted. But no sound came from them.

"Marry me, Elizabet!" The proposal rolled from his lips before he could catch it. But as soon as he said it, he knew he wanted it more than he wanted his next breath. "Wed with me now," he begged her.

She stared up at him, dumb in the face of his plea.

"I swear to God above that I will care for you above all."

Her hand flew to her breast. "How can we?"

He reached out to grasp her hand and pulled her up to face him. He wanted this more than life itself, and he wanted her to look straight into his eyes and know that he meant every word he spoke. "We needn't say our vows before a priest to make them true, my love."

She knelt before him, looking beautifully bewildered, and he took her face into his hands and kissed her with all the feeling he could invoke. He wanted her to feel his heart, wanted to bathe her in adoration.

"Marry me," he whispered against her ear.

Elizabet shuddered at the warmth of his breath against her face.

She wanted to wed him . . . wanted to love him.

Who would have thought she'd come to this place only to find love? Her dreams had been of freedom . . . but in his arms, the thought of matrimony no longer felt like a sentence, more like a beautiful promise.

"I gi' ye my word to wed you properly later if 'tis your wish, but share these vows with me now, Elizabet, and I will do my best to make you happy."

Her head spun over his proposal. Her thoughts reeled. She had never intended to marry—not ever! It had been her father's wish for her to find a husband, not her own. Broc was asking her to give up her independence. In return he was offering his love and protection. She had no doubt he would protect her, and in that instant, as she looked into his eyes, she had no doubt he would love her, as well.

Not every marriage had benefit of clergy. She knew that, though once upon a time she had dreamed of an elaborate wedding at which she and her lover would be lifted on high after their nuptials and carried to their wedding bower with shouts of good favor. But those dreams had long ago been shredded by reality. Love existed only in troubadours' tales.

Or did it?

This man standing before her claimed to hold her in his heart. Dared she believe him?

He waited for her answer, his emotions evident in his eyes.

How would she explain to everyone later? *Oh, and by the by, I married my captor.* Her brother would think her mad! And yet . . . if she were mad, indeed, then it must be with love, because she wanted this.

She couldn't think of anything that would make her happier than to sleep every night in Broc's arms.

Her heart pounded against her ribs.

She nodded, swallowing.

He took her hand in his, looking into her face, his blue eyes sincere. "I wed thee, Elizabet, and pledge you my love and swear to honor and cherish you until the day I die."

She blinked at his words, amazed he had spoken them. It seemed a sweet, crazy dream. "You . . . love me . . . truly?"

He nodded without hesitation, his eyes full of ardor. "I love you truly."

Her heart filled with his words, and her eyes with tears. The moment was far sweeter in its simplicity than any ceremony could possibly have been.

He knelt before her, totally bared, even his heart, for it was visible in his eyes. And he was magnificent in all his glory.

She swallowed, and said in return, "I wed you, Broc . . . and pledge you my love . . . and swear to honor and cherish you until the day I die."

He bent to kiss her lips, whispering softly against them, "I take you as my wife from this day onward."

She sighed. "I take you as my husband from this day onward."

He smiled at her then, and they knelt there, facing each other, feeling slightly awkward.

"What now?" Elizabet asked him.

He chuckled softly and peered down at the

erection that unyieldingly spanned the distance between them.

Elizabet bit her lip to keep from laughing at the lift of his brows.

"The wee lad would like some attention," he told her.

Wee lad was hardly the correct description for it.

It was Elizabet's turn to lift her brows. Smiling shyly up at him, she reached down to grasp the hem of her gown. And taking a deep breath, she lifted it up over her head. She didn't have to ask for his help. The gown was whisked away and tossed aside faster than she had time to part her lips.

"Christ you are lovely, woman!"

So was he, but she couldn't speak to say so. The heat of his gaze left her disarmed. His blue eyes smoldered with desire, sweeping the length of her body from her eyes to her limbs, lingering lustfully upon her breast and lower . . .

Her breath caught, and her throat felt suddenly too thick to speak. Her nipples hardened, and her body trembled. Without another word, he reached out to touch a finger to that intimate place between her thighs.

She nearly cried out with the shocking heat of his fingertip. He bent to take her mouth, then, and slid his tongue between her lips. At the same time, he slipped a scalding finger between those lips down below. The sensation of it left her dizzy, and her knees might have given way beneath her, save that he caught her in his arms, kissing her passionately . . . touching her gently . . . pressing deeper with each stroke.

"My God!" she cried breathlessly.

Her heart leapt higher with every caress.

He pulled her closer then and deepened the kiss, plunging his tongue within and ravaging her mouth with an intensity that left her weak.

"Give me your tongue," he demanded. "Kiss me back, Elizabet . . . taste me."

She did as he asked, her eyes closing in pleasure.

Broc held himself in his hand, caressing her with the tip of his shaft, reveling in the wetness she showered upon him. In that instant, as he stroked himself between her moist, sweet lips, he craved the tightness of her body beyond madness. It was all he could do not to push himself inside her. But he'd felt her maidenhead, and he wanted her first time to be pleasurable.

He wanted her wet . . . and wanting . . . wanted to lay her back upon the pallet and drink the nectar of her body.

She was limp in his arms, offering herself without reservation, gifting him with the most glorious prize ever bestowed upon man.

Groaning with desire, he laid her down upon

the pallet, kissing her lips until they were as wet and swollen as her flower.

She didn't protest, and his hands found her breasts of their own accord. She arched into them, and his body shuddered in response. Christ, it was not easy to restrain himself. It had been far too long since he'd spilled his seed into a woman.

He nibbled her breasts, then, seeking her sweet dew, lapped downward along the gentle curve of her belly, his heart hammering with anticipation.

His body shattered at the first taste of her, his heart constricting painfully as she spread her legs and arched her body, offering him a magnificent banquet.

The taste of her was like nothing he'd ever imagined, the scent of her like sweet pollen. He tasted her feverishly, suckling the bud of her desire, tugging it gently into his mouth as he had with her nipples. She cried out, lifting her legs over his shoulders, and he swore to God he would die where he lay.

"You . . . taste . . ." He forced himself away from her sweet bounty, replacing his lips with his fingers, while he nibbled and kissed his way back to her mouth. ". . . so good," he finished, offering her his tongue.

His body shuddered violently as she took him into her mouth.

It was the most wicked invitation, but Elizabet was too oblivious with desire to protest his offer. She suckled his tongue, tasting herself on his lips . . . his mouth . . . while his fingers danced the most erotic dance she had ever dreamed of.

Every nerve in her body felt alive to his touch, every breath she took a shuddering breath, every tremor she felt a quiver of ecstacy.

She was helpless beneath the onslaught of sensation. Even if she'd known what to do in return, she wouldn't have had the sense to do it, so oblivious was she.

"Spread your legs for me, my love . . ."

Moaning softly, Elizabet did as she was told, spreading her legs so that his fingers could better dance within her. She panted softly, her heart jolting with every single touch he bestowed upon her. His kisses were rapturous, his caresses shocking, but she shamelessly delighted in every glide of his fingers.

He lifted his hand suddenly to their mouths and pressed wet fingers between their joined lips, lapping them lustfully. It shocked her merely an instant, and then she joined him, her heart pounding fiercely against her ribs. Her legs spread of their own accord, seeking something, though she knew not what.

And then suddenly she felt the pressure between her legs, and she cried out, arching instinctively, impaling herself joyfully upon his body. His own cry was ragged against her ear. His body shuddered in answer, and he growled huskily, holding her closer. The pain was minimal, and the sound of his pleasure only heightened her own.

Wrapping her arms about his neck, she moved her body, undulating beneath him, needing him deeper . . . and deeper . . . deeper.

Something within her belly began to coil, spiraling its way toward a center of sensation so great in intensity that it nearly stopped her heartbeat. With every stroke of his body inside her, the thread of pleasure intensified.

And then time seemed to stand still for an interminable instant, and she felt her body climax. Her consciousness shattered into a thousand brilliant pieces in that glorious instant, and she cried out, trembling in exultation.

He answered her cry with one of his own and thrust himself one last time so deep within her that she felt him pulse against her very heart. She cried out with him, her body convulsing again.

He placed a hand at her bottom and rolled to one side, spent, dragging her with him, until she lay replete atop him, still intimately joined with his body. Her own body still pulsed with pleasure, drawing from him every last drop of his seed.

The sound of whimpering penetrated her consciousness. She peered at Harpy, who sat staring at them, whining anxiously, her expression full of curiosity. Somehow, the realization that her mother's dog had witnessed every shameless display of affection left her cheeks hot.

Harpy tilted her head, peering at their naked, entwined bodies.

"Oh, my God!" she exclaimed. Her face flushing with mortification, she buried her head against Broc's neck.

He laughed softly, the sound of his laugh wholly sated and relaxed. His hand went to her nape, massaging it gently. "Next time, we'll put the dog outside," he promised, and kissed her gently on the cheek, then hugged her sweetly.

Elizabet had never felt more cherished than she did at that moment. Her heart felt so big that it no longer seemed to fit within her breast.

She had no regrets.

None at all.

She closed her eyes, vowing to make Broc the best wife he could possibly hope for. She would learn to cook and clean, care for him. She would bear his children and raise them with love. They would have a mother and father who adored them—and never, ever find themselves without.

She only hoped—prayed—that her brother would be as pleased for her as she was.

She dozed with her face in the crook of Broc's shoulder while he stroked her back and combed his fingers through her hair.

Vaguely, she was aware that Harpy gave one last whine and then lay down beside them, relaxing as surely as Elizabet was falling asleep.

"I'm going to make everything right, Elizabet," she thought she heard him whisper, but she was far too satiated to ask precisely what he meant, and then her body eased her into a blissful state of slumber.

Chapter 21

The damage was more than apparent in the morning light. The stable had burned to the ground. The barracks behind it was half ravaged. It was going to take hard work to restore them and funds that Piers didn't have on hand.

"We'll help however we may," Leith assured him.

Piers nodded appreciatively. He had begun to make progress toward building a friendship with Meghan's brothers—more with Colin than with Leith, but Leith was probably the most honorable of the three. Gavin was virtuous but too blinded by his piety, and Colin had been, until Seana, far too concerned with his personal pleasures. Piers felt closest to Colin, because despite his covetous ways, he was the most personable and most genuine of the Brodie brothers. And there was hope for the man, at last, as Seana seemed to have brought him to his knees. It was clear to everyone who knew them that he was in love with his new bride.

"Count me in, as well," Gavin offered.

"I appreciate the offer," he told the brothers.

It was the second time Leith had pledged his men to help Piers rebuild. The first time had been to repair his fence. He was beginning to feel a sense of guilt. Someday he was going to have to return the favor. He just hoped for both their sakes that it wouldn't be soon.

Colin stood beside him, considering the demolished building with narrowed eyes. It was obvious he was lost in thought, because he wasn't the least aware of the conversation. Seana came up behind him, wrapping her arms about his waist, and he was scarce aware of her until she laid her head upon his shoulder.

He peered over his shoulder at her, and she smiled wanly.

"Meghan told me what happened."

Colin nodded.

She turned to Piers then and said, "I'm so sorry."

"'Tis hardly your fault, Seana. Where is Meghan?" Seeing the intimacy between Colin and Seana made him yearn for his own wife.

"Tending to David. The lad is a stalwart young fellow."

Piers nodded. "That he is."

"Have you any notion who burned the stables?"

Piers was glad Tomas wasn't in his presence at the instant. He would hardly accuse the man without proof, but he trusted his gut, and his gut said the man was foul. "None," he replied, and had to clench his teeth to keep from sharing his suspicions.

Colin met his gaze, his blue eyes without glimmer. Piers caught in him a sense of turmoil. Without a word, Colin turned again to stare at the ruins, and Piers reproached himself. Christ, he was beginning to see conspiracy in every glance. And yet he sensed Colin knew something he wasn't saying.

Still, he was hardly prepared to confront him when the peace they had established between them was so new. Meghan would never forgive him if he hurled accusations at any of her brothers without evidence to support his charges. Colin was a good man. If there was aught he had to reveal, he would come to Piers of his own accord.

Piers was counting on it.

In the meantime, he had set two guards to watch Tomas at a distance, as he was near certain Tomas was somehow at the center of all that had transpired. His arrival seemed to have precipitated everything.

"I'm not feeling verra well," Seana said suddenly. Her husband turned to her at once. "I think mayhap I should go home."

"Like hell you will!" he barked. "You're not going anywhere alone!"

"We don't need you at the moment," Piers assured Colin. "Take her home if she wishes to go."

He shook his head stubbornly. "I feel 'tis my duty to stay. And if I remain, so does she!"

She lifted her chin, standing tall. "Dinna be silly, Colin!" she chastised him. "It's not far to walk, and it's certainly not as though I havena traveled these woods all my life! Do ye think that in the few days since we've been wed that I've suddenly turned into an invalid?"

He frowned at her reproach but seemed to consider her words.

"I will be fine to go alone," she assured him, her tone leaving no doubt as to the strength of her determination. Piers smiled appreciatively, wholly pleased that he was not the only man to be plagued by willful, troublesome wenches.

Colin's expression remained harried, his fears obviously not alleviated, but it was clear from Seana's stance that she was not going to back down.

Her expression continued to challenge him.

Colin arched a brow at her and smiled slightly,

obviously believing he'd found a deterrent. "On one condition," he told her.

She lifted her own brow. "And what may that be, husband?"

"That you ride, not walk." The request took her momentarily aback, and he smirked at her just a little. "Take my mount," he offered, a little too sure of himself.

Piers might have warned him against being too cocky. Such tactics never worked with Meghan.

For an instant, Seana didn't respond, and then she replied, more determined than ever, "Verra well, husband." She smiled back at him, returning his smirk. "I'll ride."

"Good Christ, Seana!" Colin exploded. "You dinna even like horses!"

She winked at him. "I suppose now is as good a time as any to learn to like them. Dinna ye think?" And with that, she turned to go, and Colin bounded after her, trying in vain to talk her out of leaving.

Gavin peered at his eldest brother with lifted brows, and Leith cast a glance at Piers. The three of them shared a rare laugh together.

"That's what ye get for choosing flesh over spirit," Gavin reproached them both.

Leith ignored his rebuke. "She doesna look verra ill to me," he commented.

In truth, she didn't look ill to Piers, either, but

he said nothing, as it wasn't his place to comment.

He had enough to worry about with his own woman—not to mention Elizabet's disappearance, John's death and a stable that had been burned to the bloody ground. And if he didn't repair the damned barracks this afternoon, his men were going to be sleeping outside his bedroom door.

Only one thing made his temper more sour than Tomas's presence in his house, and that was the prospect of spending his private time with Meghan with thirty-three pairs of ears outside his door.

"Let's get to work," he suggested.

Colin could damned well handle his own affairs without an audience.

Broc scarce slept.

He didn't even close his eyes until the candle extinguished itself. He hadn't dared move, lest she awaken and leave him. It had all seemed such an exquisite dream, and if he was dreaming, he damned well didn't want to wake.

Harpy had other ideas.

The dog buried its wet nose in his ear. The shock of it startled him. The animal seemed to grin down at him, satisfied with his reaction.

"Willful dog!"

Elizabet stretched atop him, turning a beautiful smile on her belligerent dog. "What are you doing to Broc, you silly dog?" she asked it, as though she expected an answer. She yawned prettily.

"She's competing for your attention," Broc told her, grinning.

"Nay," Elizabet argued, reaching up to kiss him sweetly upon the lips. His heart swelled with joy over the gesture. "I think she's fallen in love with you, too," she said, and the implication made him smile.

"Do ye think so?"

"How could she help it? You won me over, and I am far more impervious!"

"Are you?" Broc asked her and dumped her at his side before she had a chance to respond. He rolled atop her, caressing her brow, admiring the silky perfection of her face. "I dinna believe you, lass."

"Aye, 'tis true," she swore, closing her eyes. Her lashes lay thick upon her cheeks, and he bent to kiss her reverently upon the lips, hardly believing the completeness he felt in her arms.

Never in his life had he felt so fulfilled.

"Kiss me again," she demanded sleepily, wrapping her arms about his neck.

Broc didn't need to be asked twice.

With a growl of pleasure, he pressed his

mouth to hers, and she responded by entwining her legs around his.

He made love to her then with all his heart and soul, knowing that far too soon it would be time for him to go.

Chapter 22

Seana was certain there was something amiss with Broc, and she was bound and determined to discover what it was. She urged Colin's horse into a canter.

If she could help him, she surely would. She owed him that much, after all he had done for her. She didn't like to keep anything from Colin, but for his own good, she felt it best to deal with this alone.

She'd left her husband rebuilding the barracks with his brothers and Piers. Together with their men, she had no doubt they would restore the building in little time. But the day would be long, and the search for Elizabet would be postponed until the morrow—which meant John would be buried without her. There was no way they could wait another day. But they might not have to, because she had a suspicion where the girl had gone.

It had struck her as odd that Broc would come calling so late at night and then to ask her if she ever visited the hut. And given the description of the girl's captor, it didn't take a bloody genius to determine that Broc had taken her to the hut.

The question was why.

She didn't believe for an instant that Broc would harm the girl. Nor did she believe Broc had killed Elizabet's brother. Something was not right with that picture. Broc would never harm a soul, unless in self-defense. But something had happened, and Seana was going to ask Broc straight to his face before someone else was hurt.

She was almost certain Colin suspected Broc was responsible for the girl's abduction, and he was suffering enough to keep his silence. She knew her husband felt torn. He loved Broc as a brother, but he was bound to honor Meghan's husband. She didn't want to add to his burdens. It was best he not discover where she had gone.

She considered dismounting when she was far enough away but decided it was best not to. She needed all the time she could get. It wouldn't be long before Colin came after her.

If he chanced to go home and found her missing, he would know at once where she had gone.

And sweet Christ, she didn't wish to see his anger this soon in their marriage. The sooner she faced Broc and returned home, the better for everyone involved.

Broc somehow had to make things right.

He left the hut and Elizabet along with Harpy under the pretense of going to get food. With her belly grumbling, Elizabet hadn't questioned it. He'd kissed her good-bye at the door and had left quickly, confident that she would be safe alone this morn. With the fire the previous night, he was certain Piers would have his hands too full to search for her. And Tomas didn't know the area. He wouldn't have a clue where to look.

He knew they couldn't continue as they were.

He didn't kill John, but he didn't know how to prove it at this point. His best course of action was to take Elizabet away from this place until he could think of a way to prove his innocence— if she would come with him. There was more at stake here than his relationship with Elizabet or even her life. The hard-won peace between the clans was in danger of being shattered.

He intended to speak with Iain to see what his laird advised. He didn't wish to involve Iain, but he was his last resort. He respected Iain's opinion and knew his laird would never guide him wrong.

If he remained, and Tomas accused him, their clans would be divided. If he left, hopefully with Elizabet, he might somehow convince her that he wasn't responsible for John's death, and if she forgave him for lying to her, mayhap there was hope for happiness for the two of them. He would take her to where he was born, to where his mother and father had died. Mayhap even auld Alma was still alive.

He didn't know what he was going to do, but he knew damned well he couldn't continue to do nothing. Elizabet was too perceptive to allow him to keep putting her off. Sooner or later, she was going to march into Piers' hall all by herself to get the answers he wasn't giving her.

But he was uncertain how to prove Tomas's guilt.

And he suddenly had so much to lose.

He had Elizabet.

Iain would know what to do, he hoped. At least Iain would advise him honestly, with the clan's interests foremost in his heart.

But neither would he simply hand Broc over to Piers, as Colin might feel compelled to do.

Iain didn't owe Piers anything, though Colin might feel he did. Deep in his heart, Broc didn't believe Colin would betray him, but their friendship had been sorely strained, he sensed, simply by his appearance at Colin's home. It had been made clear to Broc that night that though Colin felt a loyalty to Broc, his family—Seana and Meghan—was his greatest priority.

If only there was some way to prove Tomas

had the money pouch still and he intended to keep it. If only Broc could prove Tomas was willing to kill for it.

But Broc couldn't prove anything at all. He had to rely solely on the credit of his word. He had to trust in the simple fact that his friends and kinsmen knew him well and knew he was no liar. God's truth, he had never lied a day in his life.

Until now.

The disgusting truth was that if he confronted the bastard outright, Tomas would need only say he was holding the pouch until Elizabet was found. After all, if Elizabet were found dead, the monies would be returned to her father, not Piers.

It was that whoreson's word against his own.

And at the heart of it all was the simple fear that Elizabet would not believe him.

And why should she?

He *had* lied to her.

He prayed to God that Iain would know what to do, because his choices were few, and he didn't want to lose her now—not now that he'd only just found her.

He would do anything to keep her and keep her safe.

Anything.

Everything was different now that she was his wife.

She was his priority.

Nothing took precedence over her—not even his loyalty to Iain MacKinnon. He had bound himself to Elizabet, and whether she chose to believe in him or no, he would honor the vows they had spoken until the day he last closed his eyes.

He hadn't worn his new tunic, but Elizabet decided it probably wasn't the wisest thing he might have done anyway. If Tomas, or anyone else who knew one of them, for that matter, had spied Broc wearing the rich, red fabric, they would have known at once how to find her. She folded the tunic neatly and placed it upon the table, lovingly smoothing the wrinkles from it.

She smiled at the ridiculousness of her situation. She was just about as happy as a woman could be, considering she was being stalked by a cold-hearted murderer and stuck in a dirty hovel while she waited for her life to straighten itself out. But she was, indeed, happy—happier than she'd ever been.

Broc would fix everything, she was certain.

Sighing, she turned to lean on the table and stare at the pallet they had shared. He had touched her body so wickedly, but his tender kisses had made everything seem so right and so pure.

And his vows had been the most romantic notion she had ever heard. Certainly she had never imagined it would happen to her—and not with the most practical man she had ever met. But her wedding was surely the sort of thing of which dreams and legends were made.

She didn't need to wed him before an altar. Their communion had been one of the heart. And their witness had been the only witness that truly mattered . . . God.

Unless they wished to consider Harpy.

She blushed at the mere memory of it, but the truth was that that dog had probably witnessed far more than Elizabet could possibly imagine. After all, it had been her mother's dog.

And she, in truth, was her mother's daughter, because if she would be honest with herself, she had to confess that she had reveled in every moment they had shared last night . . . and this morning.

A wry smile turned her lips.

She must remember to thank Tomas for trying to kill her. If it hadn't been for him, Broc would never have taken her, and she wouldn't be so blessedly happy now. She was quite certain that hadn't been his intention—the rotten knave! The first thing she was going to do was tell her father. If Margaret had any knowledge of her brother's actions, Elizabet hoped her father would strangle her in his bed. If he didn't, if he was so weak that he still could not see her black heart, then so be it. Elizabet didn't need him. He hadn't taken any part in her childhood, and she didn't need him to be a part of her life now. The best thing he had done for her was to send her away with her dowry intact, and for that alone she was grateful.

She glanced down at the floor, spying a bundle under the chair, and bent to retrieve it. It had to belong to Broc, because it hadn't been there yesterday. He must have dropped it the night before during their embrace.

She set it down upon the table, wondering about its contents, and then, curious, she picked it up once more and unwrapped it.

After all, she was his wife now, and he shouldn't keep secrets from her. She smiled at that, certain she would never tire of thinking of herself that way.

Aye, she was his wife now.

The smile left her face as she opened the napkin and examined its contents. Food. Hard cheese. Bread. Nothing that would have spoiled. She cast a glance at the door, wondering if he'd forgotten that he'd brought it. He'd rushed out the door to get food.

Why would he do so if he already had something they could share? It wasn't a feast, by far, but it would certainly have gotten them through the morning.

She supposed he'd forgotten he had it.

She heard a sound outside the door then and

thought mayhap he'd remembered, after all. She set the napkin down and hurried to the door, freezing in her step as it opened to reveal a young woman.

Elizabet started at the sight of her.

For a moment, neither of them spoke, so stunned were they at the sight of each other.

And then the woman smiled. "My name is Seana," she revealed.

Elizabet nodded.

"I used to live here," the woman disclosed.

So she did.

The infamous Seana.

She was lovely, and Elizabet felt jealous at once, though she realized it was silly. The woman's kind green eyes studied Elizabet, her expression first one of confusion and then comprehension.

It occurred to Elizabet to be concerned. The last thing she needed was for Seana to run back to her husband and reveal their hiding place.

She wasn't sure she should disclose her name, but then decided her best course was honesty. If Elizabet were in her shoes, she would most appreciate honesty. She took a deep breath and said, "My name is Elizabet."

The woman's brows lifted only slightly, and she nodded, as though she wasn't entirely surprised by the revelation. She looked about the room, as though expecting to find someone else, and then her gaze returned to Elizabet.

"I hope you will forgive us for using your home," Elizabet offered.

Seana's brows lifted higher. "Us?"

Elizabet nodded. "Broc . . . and I."

"Is Broc . . . here?" Seana asked somewhat hesitantly.

"Not at the moment," Elizabet replied. "He went to get food."

Seana nodded. "And you are here alone?"

Elizabet smiled. "Not entirely . . . with my dog."

"I see." But her face screwed up with obvious confusion. "So you aren't being held against your will?" she asked Elizabet.

"Nay! Of course not!"

There was silence between them.

"Broc has been kind enough to help me," Elizabet assured her, not liking the expression on Seana's face. It left her feeling uneasy and somehow defensive of Broc.

"That would indeed be Broc."

" 'Tis a long story," Elizabet said, "but I suppose we owe you an explanation, since we are using your home."

Seana said nothing, merely looked at her, and Elizabet felt compelled to tell her about Tomas, his attempt to kill her, her need to hide from him until the truth could be discovered.

By the time Elizabet had finished her tale, they were both seated at the little table.

Seana reached out to grasp her hand, startling her with the gesture. "And what of your brother?" she asked Elizabet.

Elizabet shrugged. "He doesn't know where I am yet. Broc hasn't had the opportunity to speak with him, though he did speak to Piers' wife."

Seana frowned. "Meghan?"

"Aye. Do you not like her?"

Seana smiled and assured her without pause, "Nay, I love her."

Elizabet returned the smile, feeling as though mayhap she had found a friend.

"I take it she doesn't know you are here, either?"

"Broc thought it best he speak directly with Piers, and Piers, as yet, has not returned."

Seana suddenly lifted her hand to her forehead, as though she was upset by Elizabet's tale. Her expression when she looked up once more was a mixture of confusion and anger.

The anger Elizabet didn't understand.

"Who told you Piers was gone?" she asked then, sounding suddenly vexed.

"Broc, of course. Meghan told him Piers had gone to Edinburgh but that he would return soon."

Seana's voice was toneless when she responded, "Did she?"

Elizabet's brows knit with confusion. "Aye."

Sweet Jesu, she hadn't the first clue to what she had said to invoke the woman's sudden ire. Seana's tone had shifted from one of concern to petulance, and she decided the woman was moody.

She could be petulant all she wished. All that mattered to Elizabet was that she keep her confidence. "You won't tell anyone where we are, will you?"

Seana didn't reply for a moment, and then she shook her head. "I won't tell."

Elizabet breathed a sigh of relief. "Thank you!"

Seana's brow remained furrowed. "Dinna mention it," she said snappishly, and her tone of voice was disconcerting.

Was there more to their friendship than Broc had declared? She was obviously displeased with Elizabet, and Elizabet hadn't a single notion of what she had done.

She was on the verge of asking Seana what it was she had said that had offended her so, but once again the door opened, and Broc entered. Elizabet was so glad to see him that she leaped up from the table and ran to him, throwing her arms about his neck.

He hugged her, then pushed her gently away before turning his gaze toward Seana.

Elizabet felt her gut churn at the look they shared.

There was evidently much more here than met the eye.

Chapter 23

◠◡◠◡◠

The sand had run out of his glass.

Seana rose from the table, her chin lifting in challenge. She gave Broc a look unlike any she'd ever given him before—as though she suddenly thought him no better than a worm.

Broc said nothing in his defense.

What could he say?

"I would like to speak to you alone," Seana requested, her tone filled with outrage.

Elizabet tilted him a look. He took a deep breath and begged her to excuse them and then motioned for Seana to join him outside the hut. Elizabet released him, obviously confused by the request, stepping dumbly away. He turned to the door, opening it for Seana, and then cast a single backward glance at Elizabet before closing it behind him.

Her face was filled with turmoil.

"What are you doing?" Seana railed at him, when they were alone and far enough away from the door that Elizabet could not hear them.

Broc frowned, his chest heavy with torment. "I take it you know everything."

"Aye!" Seana screeched at him. "She told me everything! And you bloody well lied to that poor lass!"

He nodded, without excuse.

"Why?" she demanded of him. "That is hardly the Broc I know and love! I have never known you to lie to anyone in all our acquaintance!"

Broc shrugged, peering down at the ground.

"Why did you lie to her?"

He knew precisely what it was she was talking about. He shook his head, looking up into her eyes, his own eyes stinging with tears he refused to shed. "I dunno," he confessed. "At first it wasn't a lie. I didn't kill him, Seana."

Her eyes told him she wanted to believe him, but she didn't know what to believe.

"I didn't kill him," Broc repeated more firmly. "I didn't kill him, and if you dinna believe me, then who the bloody hell will?" It was as close to begging as Broc could come.

"I believe you," she conceded. "But you still lied to her, Broc, and she deserves to know that her brother is dead. She deserves to attend his burial."

He shook his head. "I can't let her go."

Seana narrowed her eyes at him. "Do ye love her?" she demanded to know.

There was no doubt in his mind. "I do."

"Then ye listen to me well, Broc Ceannfhionn. If ye dinna tell her the truth, then you will surely lose her!" She pointed irately at the hut. "If 'twas me in there and ye couldna be honest with me and speak the truth, I swear to God above that I would leave you and never look back!"

He knew she was advising him well, but he couldn't place Elizabet in danger. He couldn't allow Tomas to harm her. "If I let her go," he reasoned with her, trying to make her understand, "then I will place her at risk!" He couldn't have that.

"Trust in your friends," she retorted.

She wasn't being reasonable. "And if I had told Colin about this, what do ye think he would have done?"

She glared at him, straightening her shoulders, refusing to give in to him. "I've no idea, in truth," she admitted, "but I know he would never betray you. You saved his life, Broc. He would never let harm come to you—and certainly not at the word of some conniving Englishman!"

"Nay," he relented, "but he would feel as torn by the knowledge as you feel now, and I could not do that to him."

"You already did it to him, you bloody oaf!" Broc knew she spoke in anger. Her hands flew to her hips. "Do ye think he is so stupid that he hasna already figured it out?"

Broc nearly choked on his guilt. Already the conflict had begun, and he hadn't even revealed himself to Piers. But he damned well didn't regret helping Elizabet.

Had he to do it all over again, he would do the same.

"Trust in your friends," Seana begged. She reached out to touch him upon the arm, appealing to him.

"Do ye comprehend all that is at risk, Seana?" She nodded.

"If I confess to Piers, it will be the word of three Sassenach liars against my own. Who do you think he will believe?"

"I will stand up for you, Broc! Colin will stand up for you, as well! I know that without any doubt. And do ye think Iain will simply allow them to hand you over to be punished for something you did not do?"

"There will be bad blood between the clans," he said stubbornly, shrugging free of her touch. "Iain suggested I take Elizabet and leave until all is settled, and I think mayhap 'tis the right thing to do!"

Seana shook her head adamantly. "I dinna!"

"This isna your concern!" he told her, anger

clouding his thoughts. His temper flared. "You should have bloody well stayed out of this, Seana! I didna ask ye to interfere, and your husband wouldna appreciate your meddling!" He tried to temper his anger, but he felt trapped, without choices. "What do ye think he would say if he knew you were here?"

Her face fell at the veiled threat, and she was taken aback.

"You should bloody well have remained where ye belong—in Colin's godamn bed—and ye should mind your own lame-arsed affairs, woman!"

She blinked at his words, stepping back, looking wounded by his attack. Her eyes reddened and turned glassy, and her lip trembled when she spoke. "I came because of a boy I once knew. Do ye remember him? He came to me when others laughed and called me names because of my lame leg. He defended me to their faces, rebuking them all."

She was speaking of him, of their childhood, and his throat thickened with shame.

A fat tear rolled down her cheek, and she spoke with great affection and emotion. "He came to me and lifted me up and set me upon his lap and wiped away my tears. And he pledged me his friendship and swore he would be there for me whenever I needed him. Always."

Broc swallowed, his own eyes hazing.

"Do ye remember him?" she asked again, choking on her tears. "That boy knew right from wrong, Broc, and I came for him. Do ye understand?"

He couldn't answer. His throat was too clotted to speak. His eyes burned.

She turned away from him then and went to the horse she'd left tethered to a nearby tree, her old injury scarce visible but evident enough to accuse him. She untethered the horse without a word and mounted with some difficulty. He would have stepped forward to help her if he hadn't known with certainty that she would have refused him.

He knew Seana, knew her considerable pride.

When she was mounted, she turned to him at last. She urged the mount closer to him and looked down at him, her expression pained. "If ye love that woman in there, ye will tell her the truth, Broc. And ye will tell her before tonight so that she can attend her brother's funeral."

Broc said nothing, merely looked away, his gut burning.

"Tell her good-bye for me, please. I will not go back in there and face her with lies!"

He peered up at her, stubbornly keeping his silence, but knowing deep down that she was telling him the truth. He knew she believed it with all her heart.

"She's bonny and sweet and seems to adore ye. If ye tell her the truth, she just might forgive ye."

He was afraid to hope for that.

"But if ye dinna, Broc, I promise you will lose her."

And with that last admonition she left him to consider her words.

Chapter 24

Seana was right.

He was in danger of losing Elizabet, and God help him, she was the most important thing in the world to him. Without her, nothing else mattered.

His only chance to keep her was to go to Piers and reveal to him all that had happened. He had to count on Piers to protect her. He didn't care what happened to himself afterward, as long as Elizabet forgave him. Pride bedamned, he would throw himself on her mercy and pray she would find it within her heart to forgive him for his lies.

He bloody well loved her.

She hadn't asked him, as yet, what it was he and Seana had spoken of, and he was glad, because he wasn't quite ready to tell her. He lifted up the tunic she had set upon the table and shook it out, examining her handiwork. It was beautiful, the stitches neat and precise. She'd used the gold ribbon from her hair to trim the arms, neckline and hem. It was far finer than anything he'd ever owned before.

He only hoped it would fit him, because he loathed to disappoint her any more than he was going to already. He set the tunic down and turned to look at her. She stood by the door, peering out.

Another hour or so until the sun set.

One more hour before everything would change.

She looked so lovely standing there, with her long, shiny hair streaming down her back, that it momentarily took his breath away.

This could possibly be the last time he was ever alone with her. He prayed otherwise, but he wasn't stupid. He knew that once she discovered his deception, she might never forgive him for it.

His heart wrenching with torment, he walked to where she stood and placed his arms about her waist. He laid his head upon hers, adoring the feel of her in his arms.

She peered back at him, touching her face to his cheek.

"You seem distressed," she said, her expression full of concern—and mayhap a little hurt that he hadn't confided in her.

But she would know everything soon enough.

" 'Tis nought, lass," he lied one last time.

But it would be his last.

His one final deceit.

And he was going to make love to her one last time and hope that she would see into his heart, that she would feel his heart beating against her own and know that it belonged to her.

He pulled her into the hut, letting the door close behind them. She turned in his embrace, and he bent to kiss her, desperate for the taste of her lips. He nibbled them hungrily. Thrusting his hand into her silky hair, he turned her face up to his.

"Make love to me," he pleaded.

Elizabet peered up at him, her heart flipping painfully against her breast. She touched his face reverently, caressing him, loving him. "You never have to ask."

Didn't he realize?

Couldn't he tell?

Her body craved him every instant they were together. Her heart yearned for his every touch and caress.

He had been distant and brooding since Seana's appearance, and she had been afeared that he regretted their vows. There was something between the two of them, as she had suspected, but she was glad he had remained with her.

Her breath quickened as he bent to kiss her

lips, and her heart jolted excitedly as his arms enfolded her. His warm, big hands caressed her body, touching her everywhere, awakening her senses once more. He paused at her bottom, cupping his hand beneath it, and lifted it gently, his breath coming ragged in her ear.

Elizabet closed her eyes in absolute joy as he bent further to lift the hem of her gown, and all she could do was cling to his neck for support as his hands slid beneath her dress. He kissed her mouth, thrusting and tasting as she knew he would do elsewhere . . . slick and hot. And then he moved to her neck, biting gently, kissing her, and God have mercy, but she never wanted him to stop!

He dipped his face into her bosom, kissing and lapping the valley of her breasts.

The barely restrained passion in his every touch left her breathless and titillated and panting with desire.

He lifted her up and without a word carried her to the table, setting her atop it. His eyes never left her as he pushed her back on it.

Elizabet's breath caught as he lifted up her dress to unveil her to his eyes. It was one thing to reveal herself in the darkness, with a single taper lit against the night, and another entirely to do it by daylight when nothing was hidden from his eyes.

The intensity of his expression took her breath

away. He stared down at her, his chest heaving with desire, and his arms tensed at his sides.

She swallowed, and opened for him, wanting him to come inside.

She belonged to him.

He belonged to her.

And she wanted no secrets between them, no barriers, no shame.

He sucked in a breath at what she so brazenly revealed and whispered, "So verra beautiful."

With deft movements, he divested himself of his garb and then fell to his knees before her, gloriously naked, to drink of her body.

Seana arched her back, eagerly anticipating the touch of his tongue. It was warm and silky when it came at last, and she moaned with desire. He lapped her hungrily, tasting her, kissing her, and as he did, the remembered taste of herself upon his lips made her cry out.

She shuddered with exhilaration as warmth flooded through her body and he groaned at the taste of it. He stood then, looking down upon her, his eyes dark with passion. Still quivering with her climax, she opened for him, and he took himself into his hand, pushing into her body. His head fell back and he cried out in pleasure as he entered her.

He made love to her until she came to a second climax and then a third, until she thought he would never stop, until she trembled beneath him one last time, sobbing with joy.

And then he gave a final, violent thrust and shuddered with his own release.

"I love you," he cried out. "I'm sorry . . . I'm sorry . . ."

She thought he meant he was sorry for hurting her, but he hadn't hurt her at all. She reached out to embrace his head to her bosom, reassuring him, lacing her fingers through his hair, cooing softly to him.

" 'Tis alright," she whispered, stroking the hair from his damp face. "Everything is going to be alright."

Nothing was going to be alright.

Broc dressed himself in the tunic Elizabet had fashioned for him, grateful that it fit. He wrapped himself afterward in his plaid, praying she would believe him.

"Bring the dog," he directed, his heart squeezing painfully.

"Where are we going?" she asked when he took her by the hand and led her out of the hut.

"To speak with Piers," he replied, his tone dull. He tried to make his mouth say the rest, but he couldn't get the words past his lips.

The expression on her face was one of surprise. "He's returned from Edinburgh?"

"Aye," he answered simply and fell into silence beside her, holding her hand. Harpy, tail wagging, kept pace at her side.

"I see," she said low and must have sensed his turmoil, because she suddenly looked distressed. He thought she might be afeared, as well.

"I won't let anything happen to ye," he promised. "Dinna be afraid, Elizabet."

She nodded, and he gently squeezed her hand in reassurance.

God help him, he didn't know how to say it.

There seemed no good time. He'd never intended to wait until they reached Piers' manor before breaking the news to her, but in the contemplative silence, the walk seemed far too short, and before he realized, they had arrived.

It was near dark now, and the burned remains of the stable sat like an open wound upon the land. He led her toward the sound of the reed in the distance, its song melancholy.

Everyone had gathered in the field near the little chapel.

"It looks like a funeral," she remarked, peering up at him.

His heart pounding painfully, he pulled her toward the gathering, never daring to look at her.

They reached the church before the gathering. Before it sat a simple white cross wrapped in Brodie plaid.

God forgive him, but this instant, he almost

wished it were himself being laid in the ground.

How was he going to face her after?

With every step he took, his stout legs seemed as though they would falter.

"Forgive me," he begged her.

Elizabet was beginning to get the most terrible feeling in the pit of her belly.

Broc's face was pale, his expression full of regret. Confusion enveloped her.

She stopped and turned to face him. "Forgive you . . . for what?"

He wouldn't look at her. He tried but couldn't meet her eyes. He turned away to peer at the gathering of people in the distance, his throat bobbing.

He shook his head and said only one word, "John."

But clarity returned with that single utterance. She turned toward the crowd in the distance, comprehension dawning.

"No!" she exclaimed, her heart thumping against her ribs. He remained silent, and she tore her hand from his grasp. "Tell me it isn't so!" she demanded of him.

He didn't speak, wouldn't look at her.

She flew at him, pounding him on the chest. Harpy began to bark.

"No!" she screamed.

She turned from him and began to run toward the gathering, shouting her brother's name.

Harpy ran after her, barking at her heels. In the distance, the music ended, and she ran blindly toward the crowd, which turned to face her, watching her approach. She felt as though her legs would give way.

It couldn't be so.

God, please tell me it isn't so! she demanded, and began to cry. He couldn't be dead.

But he was.

Tomas noticed her first and came striding toward her, the look in his eyes dark and frightening, but she wasn't afeared. He wouldn't dare touch her in front of so many people. His tone didn't seem to match his expression.

"Elizabet!" he called out, sounding relieved to see her. "Dear God, where have you been?"

She ran past him, pushing his arms away from her as she stumbled through the crowd, meeting Seana's familiar gaze. The woman's expression was filled with pity, and Elizabet cried out in grief at what she was beginning to comprehend.

Tears blurred her vision.

Faces began to melt before her eyes.

"Elizabet!" shouted one of her father's men. She recognized his voice but didn't see his face.

She stumbled to her knees beside the gaping hole in the ground. Beside her, some man stood frozen at his task, dirt piled high upon his shovel, ready to throw it down into the open grave. Blind anger surged up from the depths of her, and she shoved him away.

"John!" she sobbed, staring down into the black hole. He was already half covered with soil.

Someone came forward and tried to comfort her. Someone else came and dragged her to her feet.

She felt suddenly dizzy. Everything faded as though it were nought but a terrible dream.

The last thing she remembered before blackness fell over her was Broc's face as he came toward her.

Chapter 25

Elizabet sat weeping at Montgomerie's table. Seana and Meghan stood at her back, both trying to soothe her.

"If she wishes to go home, 'tis her right to go," Tomas said in her defense.

Piers remained unyielding. "Her father sent her to me, and I'll not simply turn her about and send her home!"

Piers sat across from her, watching Tomas pace angrily before the table, but she was weeping too hard to express her wishes.

What a fool she had been!

How could she have believed in Broc? What was wrong with her that she should throw herself at the first man who showed her any attention.

He wasn't really the first man, she amended,

307

but he was certainly the first from whom she'd welcomed the attention.

Colin and his brothers had dragged Broc away, shouting and cursing at them to let him go. They'd had to pin him down and speak to him in low tones. Elizabet was told that he had agreed to leave, only if Piers promised that Elizabet would not be left alone in Tomas's care.

But it wasn't his right to request such a thing. She repudiated him as her husband. Their vows had not been spoken before God.

It didn't matter that in her heart she had felt every last word. She would always bear the painful memory of their brief time together. She had wanted so very much to believe in him.

"You don't believe that idiot Scot!" Tomas shouted in anger.

"I don't know what to believe," Piers said.

Tomas must have stamped his foot in protest. Elizabet glanced up to find his face mottled with anger.

"You have two witnesses who swear they saw that damned savage kill John before their very eyes. Will you call them both liars, Montgomerie?" Tomas asked him.

Piers' expression turned cold. "I have called no man a liar," he said tonelessly, tapping his fingers restlessly upon the table.

"Aye, but you have!" Tomas argued.

Piers stood.

"Piers," Meghan said at her back.

He glanced at his wife, his eyes dark with anger, his temper barely restrained.

"If you would believe that Scot devil rather than two of your God-fearing countrymen, then you have named them liars!"

Piers cast his head back, obviously trying to control himself, but Elizabet wanted Tomas to win this argument. He was right. How could they believe Broc, when two witnesses saw him murder her brother in cold blood?

Broc had lied to her.

To her very face he had lied to her.

She wanted to go home.

If her father would not allow her to remain in his house, then she would take her dowry and place herself in a nunnery. There she would spend the remainder of her life.

She didn't ever wish to open her heart again! She didn't want ever to wed anyone else! She didn't want to believe in any man's lies!

Nor did she appreciate these two pompous men discussing her as though she weren't even present. Didn't her wishes count for anything?

"I want to go home," she said softly. Both men turned to look at her, and she sat straight in the chair.

"Elizabet," Seana protested.

Elizabet shrugged away from her, casting her a wounded glance. Seana hadn't precisely lied to her, but she had allowed Elizabet to continue to believe something that wasn't true. She might have spoken up and kept Elizabet from making a fool of herself.

What a fool Seana must have thought her rambling on and on about Broc, about their vows, about love.

The very thought of it stung her eyes once more. Her heart wrenched painfully.

She never ever wanted to set eyes upon that man again. The sooner she left this place, the better she would feel.

She stood, facing Piers squarely. "I wish to go home!" she repeated adamantly.

He shook his head, stubbornly refusing her. "I cannot allow that, Elizabet."

Anger suffused her. She squared her shoulders, challenging him. She didn't care who he was. He had no right to make decisions for her.

"You cannot allow it?"

His expression remained unyielding. He said nothing, refusing to be baited, but Elizabet wasn't going to accept his decree so easily.

This was her life.

"Are your loyalties so twisted, my lord, that you would keep your promise to a liar over your obligation to your own flesh and blood?"

"You are out of line, Elizabet," he told her, though his tone was gentle.

"Nay, my lord! You are out of line!" she countered, unwilling to cede to him. "This is my life, and my decision to make, and I wish to go home!"

Tears streamed from her eyes. She couldn't stop them.

His eyes slanted with compassion.

"If you do not allow her to return with me," Tomas interjected, his lip curving into a smirk, "I will be certain to tell Geoffrey that you took the word of a Scots bastard over that of his daughter and two witnesses. That man murdered his son, and you refuse even to punish him for his crime. The least you can do is let this poor girl go home to her father. She has been abused more than enough."

Piers sighed, relenting. It was clear he didn't wish to let her go, but Elizabet was determined. He ignored Tomas's ultimatum and said to her, "Are you certain 'tis your wish to go, Elizabet?"

Elizabet nodded, grateful that he would consider her request. "I cannot stay here," she assured him and began to sob. "I cannot stay!" she cried out and left the table.

If she didn't leave their presence at once, she was going to disgrace herself with tears. She ran to the staircase, weeping, desperate to be away from so many pairs of eyes.

"We will leave in one hour," she heard Tomas say to Piers as she raced up the stairs. "Ready yourself, Elizabet!" he shouted after her.

Broc sat in Colin's hall, surrounded by the three brothers. They'd convinced him to leave Elizabet in Piers' care, but he was afraid they would let her go with Tomas.

He buried his face in his hands, trying to block the image of Elizabet's accusing face from his memory. His heart felt near to bursting with grief. And he kept seeing the pain in her expression as she'd turned from her brother's grave to face him. She'd swooned then, and he'd lifted her up at once and carried her to Piers' hall.

Tomas, the bastard, had demanded his immediate arrest, and they'd rent her out of his arms.

As long as he lived, he would never forget that look of betrayal upon her face.

He'd promised not to let her down, and he had done far worse than that. He'd lied to her and more . . . he'd left her in Tomas's hands.

He'd recognized the man at once as the bowman in the woods. There was no doubt in Broc's mind that Tomas intended her ill. But he hadn't been able to convince anyone else of that fact, not when Tomas and his lackeys all pointed their fingers at him in accusation.

He was going to kill the whoreson with his bare hands!

He stood up, fury in his stance, ready to do battle. "I have to go back!" he told them. "I canna leave her with him! Dinna ye understand?"

All three of them stood in his way, Leith, Colin and Gavin, ready to stop him if they must.

"We believe you," Leith assured him, "but 'tis the word of three against your own, Broc. What would you have had me do?"

"If you return there, you will force Piers' hand," Gavin explained.

"Be patient," Colin said. "Piers gave his word that he would not allow Elizabet to leave, and he willna betray his word. Sassenach he may be, but he is an honorable man."

Broc slammed his fist upon the table. "Do ye honestly believe he will go against his own kin and countrymen to keep his word to me?"

Leith reasoned with him. "I know only this, Broc, if ye return against his wishes, we canna defend ye any longer."

"Listen to Leith," Colin demanded of him.

They had him trapped behind the long table and surrounded on all sides. He felt like a caged lion, savage and angry, desperate to be at Elizabet's side.

What good did it do him if his friends believed

him yet he couldn't protect the woman he loved?

Fury boiled up inside him, turning his vision black. By damn, no one was going to keep him from what he knew he must do. "She's my wife!" he roared, and kicked the table before him with all his might. Its massive weight toppled from the dais, leaving the way clear for him to go.

He ran toward the door.

Only Colin was quick enough to block his exit.

"If ye know what's good for ye," he told Colin, "you'll move the bloody hell out of my way!" His fists clenched and unclenched at his sides.

Colin drew himself up to do battle with him, though Broc was far bigger than he.

Leith and Gavin were there at once at his side.

Broc looked his best friend square in the eyes and said simply, "What if it were Seana?"

They stared at each other, deadlocked, and for an instant, Colin didn't reply. His jaw clenched with indecision. He blinked then and put up his hands for Leith and Gavin to back off.

"I canna stand at your back," he told Broc, his tone vehement.

"I willna ask ye to!" Broc countered, ready to barrel his way through the door if need be, but he wanted no quarrel with Colin.

"Know that if you leave here you put me and my brothers at risk," he told Broc, and then, without another word, he stepped out of Broc's way, eyeing his brothers in a warning not to interfere, making his position clear.

Elizabet was all that mattered at the moment.

Praying he wasn't too late, he bolted at once out the door.

Chapter 26

⟡

Tomas was in a quandary.

He couldn't allow Elizabet to return to Geoffrey, but it wasn't going to be an easy task to be rid of her.

Having her at his disposal was half the battle, and he was pleased the wench had mettle enough to stand up to Montgomerie—the arrogant bastard would never have let her leave elsewise.

Still, he couldn't simply kill her. He had to do it so that it placed suspicion on his two companions. They were stupid, mayhap, but loyal to Geoffrey, so he hadn't dared approach them. They rode ahead of him, Elizabet at his side, her mood somber and her eyes red-rimmed from her ceaseless weeping.

Well, he'd be damned if he'd give up his purse. He deserved to keep it.

It was his.

So was that damned crucifix she wore like a trophy around her waist. He eyed her malevolently, his gaze drawn to the girdle she wore. The object of his concern was pressed into her hand. She held it as though it were a talisman to ward away her grief.

The look upon Margaret's face when she'd first spied the piece of jewelry had been lamentable. She'd known at once that he'd stolen the trinket from her jewel box. Though she never asked him about it, he knew she knew. Still, the look in her eyes when she discovered it on Elizabet's girdle and realized he'd used it to pay some whore for his pleasures had turned his gut.

He understood why it upset her so. It had been a gift to Margaret first . . . a lover's gesture, not a brother's.

Elizabet rode stoically at his side, saying nought, her gaze distant, and he knew she was thinking of that damned Scot.

Stupid wench.

She thought the worst was done.

Well, he was going to give her something better to weep over. She thought her life was over without him, did she? Well he had news for her. She wasn't going to need to waste her dowry on some abbess's treasury after all.

*   *   *

Broc had no choice but to appropriate one of Montgomerie's horses from the field where he'd put them.

Piers was like to be angry when he discovered it missing, but Broc didn't give a damn. Piers had broken his word. He'd looked Broc straight in the face and sworn to him that he would not leave Elizabet in Tomas's hands. Then he'd let her go anyway, abandoning her to that bastard's mercy.

He was afeared he was going to be too late.

He'd never forgive himself if anything should happen to her.

Elizabet was all that mattered to him.

Chapter 27

⌒◯◯⌒

Elizabet's heart felt as though it had been ripped from her breast. In its place was emptiness, sorrow and pain.

She had never dared to hope that she would find love and live happily ever after, but it was a cruel, cruel twist of fate that she should be taunted with a glimpse of it and then have every chance of happiness snatched from her embrace.

She didn't see how she could ever be happy again—not after Broc.

She had felt so cherished in his arms, so beautiful, so full of hope . . .

Now she felt only foolish.

Never again would she allow herself to fall prey to a man's sweet words and gentle caresses. Never would she be so stupid to place her trust in any man's care.

In fact, let any man dare even look at her sideways, and she would curse him to hell where he belonged! Men were faithless knaves, who cared only for their own selfish pleasures.

She didn't want to remember the devotion with which he had worshiped her body or the unselfish way he had made love to her. She wished she could erase the memories entirely, for she knew it would leave her aching for something she could never have.

And Tomas... she no longer saw him the same somehow. There was something in his demeanor that seemed sinister now.

Her other two companions were decent men, and she trusted their words. If it hadn't been for their testimony, she would never have taken Tomas's word over Broc's. But they had sworn by her father's honor that they had, with their own eyes, witnessed Broc's murder of John.

And the worst of it all was that she, too, had witnessed everything—except that she had been too enraptured with Broc to trust her own eyes. She had allowed him to convince her otherwise with scarce more than a wink of his blue eyes and a few empty assurances.

As it turned out, he was nought but a liar— and she was a fool because she still wanted to believe him.

She cast an annoyed glance at Tomas, wishing he would keep to himself. If she had to suffer his presence every instant of their journey home, she thought, she would scream. He was like her shadow now, never leaving her side. No matter that the other two had given testimony to his innocence, she couldn't help but feel uneasy in his company.

"You made the right choice, Elizabet."

She nodded, not wishing for conversation at the instant.

"You made the only choice to honor your brother."

Elizabet's heart wrenched at the reminder.

John deserved far more than to be buried in some foreign land by a bunch of strangers who cared nought more for him than they did for justice and truth.

"I'm only glad you were fortunate enough to escape," Tomas persisted.

She hadn't escaped, in truth. Broc had shamelessly brought her there—after having his way with her—without any warning of what she would encounter. For that, too, she would never forgive him. Though it scarce mattered, because he like as not didn't care how she felt. If he had, he would've at least honored her with the truth.

Shame kept her tongue stilled.

Fury kept her from weeping.

"He was a dangerous man, Elizabet!" Tomas said, as though rebuking her.

She cast Tomas a beleaguered glance. "You

needn't tell me what I already know!"

Sweet Jesu, she was beginning to believe that all men were bent on inflicting misery and heartache! *Go away!* she begged him silently.

"Anyone who could so savagely cut a man's throat and leave him to be mauled by the animals should be hung by his entrails!"

Bile rose in her throat at his exclamation.

"So much blood!" he said, shaking his head. "Poor young John. " 'Tis a fortunate thing you did not see him," he assured her.

Her heart jolted, and she straightened in the saddle, suddenly realizing what he'd said.

John's throat hadn't been cut. Nor had there been any blood. She recalled it clearly, because she'd searched for a wound and had found not one single drop of blood or any sign of injury. When Broc had assured her that he'd merely smacked him with the butt of his dagger, she had believed him because, in truth, she hadn't spied any wound at all.

She looked at Tomas, trying to determine whether she had heard him correctly or not. He wasn't looking at her. His gaze was fixed elsewhere, mayhap in memory.

She peered about, searching for their companions, and found that they were nowhere in sight. It was only she and Tomas. She'd been so busy castigating herself for her mistakes that she hadn't even been aware of their surroundings.

Her heart began to beat a little faster as she gathered the reins in her hands. "Where are the others?" she asked Tomas casually.

He tilted her a glance, arching a brow. "Riding ahead. Considering that we managed to get ourselves lost last time, I suggested we be certain to travel the right path."

"Good idea," Elizabet remarked, trying to sound nonchalant, though she was suddenly anything but.

"Everyone is anxious to be across the border," he explained, "and I wanted to be certain we traveled expeditiously. This land is filled with dirty savages," he told her. "Though you seemed so preoccupied that I didn't wish to harry you nor leave you alone."

Elizabet nodded, willing her heartbeat to slow. "I'm grateful," she assured him, turning her attention toward the horizon. The land was flatter now, and few trees obstructed the scenery, but there was no sign of the other two. She swallowed, telling herself to remain calm.

She cast Tomas a veiled glance, trying to determine whether he sensed her apprehension. He wore a placid smile and seemed not to have a single concern.

She carried no weapon at all, not even a dirk.

Her gaze fell to the pack that hung over his mount. He kept his crossbow there, which he used to hunt for their meals. Her belly fluttered at the realization. Broc had claimed he'd spied a bowman. Tomas was, indeed, partial to the bow. He carried no sword but kept one sheathed in the scabbard that was slung on his horse. His dagger, he kept in his belt; it was the only weapon he carried on his person.

She was beginning to get the most awful feeling in the pit of her belly.

Oh, God . . . what if Broc was right?

How could she be certain anymore who was telling the truth?

She took a deep breath and dared to ask, "I meant to inquire . . . but forgot . . . about the pouch. . . ."

Her heartbeat quickened.

"Pouch?" he said, sounding perplexed. His brow furrowed as he looked at her.

"My dowry," she reminded him. "Did you remember to take it from John's body? He was carrying it, as you recall."

"The pouch!" he exclaimed, as though only just recalling it. "Nay." He shook his head soberly. "I'm afeared it was stolen by that Scots bastard," he told her.

Elizabet lifted her brows and turned away, her breath catching painfully.

That was the one thing she knew absolutely for certain. Broc did not steal the pouch. There hadn't been time. He hadn't even known about it.

Fear squeezed her heart. It flip-flopped against her ribs. She tried to speak but couldn't. Her stomach turned violently at the impact of his disclosure, and she felt suddenly as though she would be physically and uncontrollably ill. Dizziness threatened to spill her from her mount.

God help her. Broc had been telling her the truth all along. She knew that with a sudden certainty that overwhelmed her.

And she was alone with this madman with no weapon to protect herself.

She closed her eyes, trying to compose herself, forcing her thoughts to clear, and repressed the overpowering urge to wheel her mount about and fly back to Broc.

Jesu . . .

She said a silent prayer, begging God's aid and Broc's forgiveness. It was true that he hadn't told her about her brother, but he had been speaking the truth about everything else.

Piers had tried to keep her from leaving, but she had been stubborn and willful in her anger.

She hadn't realized how long she'd been silent, until he commented on her reticence.

She shook her head. "I'm just tired, that's all," she lied.

"We've quite a way to go," he replied.

Her stomach roiled.

She had to get away from him somehow. The reins shook in her hands. There was no better time than the present. The longer they rode, the farther they would be from anyone who might help her, the less her chances for survival. She swallowed her fear and said, laughing nervously, "I'm afraid I must beg you to give me respite." She reined in her horse. "I must have a few moments of privacy."

He frowned at her. "Is aught wrong?"

"Nay!" she lied. "Nought at all." He reined in as well, and she cast him a sheepish look and said, " 'Tis merely that I must attend to my personal affairs."

His brow arched. "Can't it wait?"

She shook her head fervently. "Nay."

His scowl deepened, and he gave her a harried look. "Very well, then." He glanced about, as though surveying their surroundings.

There were no trees in the immediate vicinity, nothing to hide behind, which would work to her benefit. He couldn't possibly expect her to squat before him.

"There is a small hillock in the distance," he told her. "Why don't you ride ahead of me and attend to yourself there. I shall bide my time, and by the time I reach you, you should be done."

She looked about with a sense of growing desperation. She didn't want to ride ahead, but it seemed that she didn't have a choice. She didn't wish to cast suspicion upon herself. If she could get far enough ahead of him, then there was a chance she might be able to turn about and ride back far to his flank without him spying her.

She nodded, eager to be away from him. "Very well," she agreed. "I shall." And she gave him a nod and heeled her mount into a canter. She didn't dare turn around to look into his face, so afeared was she that he would anticipate her intentions. She rode faster, grateful not to hear hoofbeats at her back.

Please, God, she prayed, *let me get away from him.*

"Broc," she whispered, and tried to envision his face, drawing her courage from him.

Chapter 28

Tomas watched her go, his gut burning. He had begun to think mayhap he wouldn't have to kill her. After all, he didn't wish to bring suspicion upon himself. He had the money, and for now that was enough. Who could, after all, prove that Broc hadn't indeed taken it?

But something about her manner had changed. She had been quiet far too long.

Had he said something to rouse her mistrust?

Something about the way she rode away set him ill at ease.

"Elizabet!" he called after her.

She didn't stop.

"God damned bitch!" he exclaimed, fury surging through him. He slammed the heel of his boot into his mount and flew after her.

Elizabet cast a glance over her shoulder, finding her worst fears realized, and her heart flew into her throat. She urged her mount faster, no longer keeping up any pretense. As soon as she bounded over the hill and Tomas could no longer see her clearly, she began to turn at a wide angle, doubling back around. By the time he realized, she hoped it would be too late.

She bent low over her horse, racing against time, she knew. She didn't dare turn to look over her shoulder again. Praying to God that she would lose him, she rode with all her might. She closed her eyes and drove the horse to its potential, feeling the wind full in her face and hoping to God the beast wouldn't tire too quickly.

When she opened her eyes again, she had to blink twice at what she saw. At first, it was merely a dark speck on the horizon that grew with every fierce clip of her horse's hooves. When she realized what it was, she nearly cried out with joy.

It was Broc.

He rode toward her on a big black steed, looking gloriously leonine with his thick mane of golden hair flowing out behind him. He was unmistakable in the rich red tunic she had sewn for him. The sight of him stole her breath away.

As the thunder of his horse's mount grew nearer, she began to weep aloud with elation.

Sweet, merciful God!

She slowed her mount as she approached him,

unaware that she did. But he didn't stop.

"I love you!" he shouted as he passed her, his blue eyes alighting on her only for the briefest instant. He thundered past her then toward the approaching rider.

Elizabet wheeled her mount about to see her lion-hearted husband unsheathe his immense sword from his scabbard in a movement so swift and beautiful that it awed her.

Too late, Tomas fumbled with the satchel, trying to free his bow.

"Die, ye rotten bastard!" Broc shouted, as he thundered into battle.

As before, it was over before it began.

Elizabet put her hands over her eyes to shut out the terror of it. But this time, there was no mistaking the death blow. Tomas toppled to the ground, tangled in the reins. His riderless horse reared, screaming in terror, coming to its knees.

With sword still in hand, Broc wheeled his mount about, slowing as he passed Tomas's limp body. He cast it a single glance and then resheathed his sword as his gaze returned to Elizabet.

Her heart soared.

She dismounted to wait for him, eager to hold him, eager to tell him that she loved him, adored him, wanted to bear his children.

"I'm sorry!" she said as he neared. He leaped from his horse before it came to a halt, taking her breath away as he took her into his arms.

His face and tunic were spattered with blood, but she didn't care. His was the most beautiful face she had ever seen, and she wanted never to be without him again. She caressed his face, reaching up on tiptoes to kiss his mouth.

"I love you, too, my darling husband!" she declared. "Oh, God . . . can you ever forgive me?" she asked him, tears streaming down her cheeks.

He held her tightly, his heart beating fiercely against her breasts. "Only if ye promise never again to leave me!"

"Never!" she swore. "Never, my love!"

He kissed her then so passionately that it stole her breath away.

She closed her eyes and held his face in her hands, reveling in the strength of his arms.

"My beautiful lion," she declared, lacing her hands through his hair. She sighed contentedly and smiled, her heart bursting with joy. "I cannot believe you came all this way to save me!"

"Nay, lass," he countered with a crooked smile, "I came to tell ye that ye forgot your bloody dog."

Harpy!

Elizabet gasped in shock. "Oh, my God!" Her hand flew to her mouth. She had been so distraught, she hadn't even remembered her mother's poor dog. "Where is she?" she demanded at once.

He winked at her. "Just where you left her—chewing up Montgomerie's boots."

Elizabet stifled her laughter.

He lifted her up suddenly, gave her a kiss upon the forehead then walked over to her horse, setting her unceremoniously atop it. "Let's go home, wife," he said, sounding suddenly irascible.

"Aye, husband," she agreed, smiling crookedly down at him as she bent to retrieve the reins. "Let's go home."

Epilogue

~~~◦◦◦~~~

The sound of a dog's bark outside caught Elizabet's attention. She knew that bark. It brought a smile to her lips.

Heavy with child, she rose awkwardly to her feet. "Constance," she said, "watch the baby for me, darling."

She didn't have to ask twice.

Thirteen-year-old Constance was enamored with the children, doting on them. Broc's little cousin was blossoming into a lovely young woman with hair as golden as her husband's and eyes the same shade of blue as her brother Cameron's.

"Oh, yea!" Constance exclaimed, and she leapt off the bed where two-year-old Maggie lay, babbling happily at the ceiling. She had been tickling the child's feet.

Elizabet couldn't help but laugh at Constance's enthusiasm.

"Hallo, wee little Griffin!" Constance cooed at the baby. "Hallo!" She approached the child, making faces, and three-year-old Griffin happily stamped his little feet in the tub of water. He giggled when she pulled up her dress and stepped into the tub along with him.

Elizabet laughed and glanced heavenward, marveling at the course her life had taken.

Who would have thought that after growing up alone, without siblings, without even parents to speak of, she would end with two dogs, three children of her own, another on the way and an adopted daughter so sweet that she made her heart swell with joy.

"He so verra loves to be naked," Constance observed, smiling down at her shameless little dark-haired son.

"So did someone else I know," Broc assured her, as he came in the door. He stood in the doorway, watching.

"Broc!" Constance exclaimed.

"Da! da!" Griffin shouted with glee and continued to dance about in the tub, splashing water everywhere.

Elizabet turned to her husband. Her heart still quickened at the sight of him. Even after all these years, the mere sound of his voice still took her breath away.

He lifted a brow, casting Elizabet a nod, and turned back to Constance, assuring her, " 'Tis the truth that I held that bare arse of yours in my arms far too many times, lass."

"Uncle Broc!" Constance protested, making a face. "That is so verra disgusting!"

"Aye, but 'tis true, Constance. Ask your aunt Elizabet."

"Or ask Page," Elizabet suggested, greeting her husband at the door, "she chased you about far more than I."

"I dinna believe you!" Constance exclaimed. But she knew it was true, because she could not suppress her guilty grin.

Broc nodded, "Och, lass, I dinna think you wore clothes until you were twenty," he remarked.

Constance rolled her eyes, giggling at his obvious exaggeration. "But I'm only thirteen!" she declared.

Elizabet stifled her laughter and crooked a brow at her husband. "And where is Suisan?" she asked him.

He wrapped his arms around her, turning her about so that he could hug her and place his hands upon her belly. "Suisan is outside riding the dog," he disclosed.

Suisan was their eldest daughter, their first-born, conceived the night they'd first spoken their vows. She was her father's joy, and her father clearly was hers. She claimed to want to grow up to be just like her da. And at seven, she much preferred wielding sticks as swords and galloping about upon the backs of tired old dogs to hanging about her mother's skirts.

Her husband glanced over at Maggie lying upon the bed and whispered into Elizabet's ear, "Have you any notion how beautiful your children are?"

She cast him a reproachful glance. "Are they not yours, as well?"

He winked at her. "Only when they are laughing," he told her. "When they are crying, they are yours."

She rolled her eyes and smacked him upon the thigh. "You are incorrigible!"

He hugged her then, holding her close, kissing her upon the cheek. "Och, woman, mayhap so, but do ye realize how much I love ye?"

Elizabet sighed contentedly and leaned back upon her husband's chest, savoring the quiet strength of his arms. She smiled. "Not as much as I love you!"

He shook her gently, growling low. "I beg to differ, woman!" he said. "Just look at how many children I gave you!"

"I bore them," she reminded him, pointing a finger at her breast in mock offense.

He squeezed her gently. "Aye, well, I watched you bear them!" he countered, vying with her.

"You most certainly did not!" Elizabet reminded him, aghast at his prevarication. "You hid your eyes!"

He had the nerve to look wounded by her accusation. "Och," he protested, kissing her upon the ear. "Only because I could not bear to see you in pain, wife."

Elizabet laughed. That much was true. He hadn't been able to bear her screams, though he'd threatened to kill the midwife if she did not allow him to remain within the house. Despite her protest that it was unseemly, he'd paced the floor of her chamber with his hand upon his eyes. The very memory left her smiling.

"And what will you do this time?" she asked him, patting her belly.

"I will not leave your side," he swore. "Even if you curse me with every breath."

Elizabet laughed. "I would never!"

He gave her a mock sigh. "Ah, but you did. You told me you'd rather I were a bugger and that if I dared ever touch you again you would wrap me up in my ba—"

Elizabet slapped him before he could speak it aloud before the children. Constance, for one, was listening with interest to their banter.

He bent to rest his chin upon her shoulder and patted her belly, too. "Any regrets?"

She shook her head with certainty. "Not a one."

"I'm glad," he whispered, and the warmth of his breath at her ear sent a shiver down her spine. "I'm a verra, verra happy man," he declared.

And to think she might never have known how wonderful it was to be part of a family. Elizabet glowed in his affection. Whenever she thought of how close she'd come to losing him, it still saddened her. But as soon as such thoughts dared enter her mind, all she needed to do was look into the faces of her children or consider the gentle warmth of their home, and all melancholy thoughts were instantly banished.

Her dowry had built them a fine little house, and though she wasn't surrounded by luxuries, her table was always laden with food and her house filled with laughter and friends.

And she was blessed with the greatest gift of all—love.

What greater reward in life was there than that?

The door opened suddenly, and in bounded Harpy along with Suisan. Suisan ran at once to the bed, leaping upon it to tickle her baby sister on the belly.

Harpy trotted over to Elizabet, wagging her tail wearily, no doubt grateful for the respite.

Elizabet patted her lovingly and silently thanked her for leading her to Broc. She sent another prayer of gratitude heavenward.

After all, if her husband hadn't once attempted to steal her mother's dog, she wouldn't be standing here now with his loving arms around her.

Thank God for wayward dogs.

THE HUSBAND LIST
BY
VICTORIA ALEXANDER

Lady Gillian Marley's Husband List

1. Viscount Reyonlds—a gambler and worse, unsuccesful.
2. The marquis of Dunstable—pleasant enough, but with nine children more in need of a governess.
3. Lord Tynedale—remarkably well spoken for a man with few teeth.
4. Baron Raitt—charming gentleman, though advanced age has left its mark.
5. Lord Clevis—excellent dancer in spite of proportions that shake the foundations of any house with his first steps upon the floor.

The earl of Shelbrooke

A rake, entirely too handsome but apparently quite reformed.

And we all know there is no better husband than a reformed rake.

Dear Reader,

What if you had to get married but there were no good prospects in sight? That's the problem facing Lady Gillian in Victoria Alexander's newest Regency-set historical THE HUSBAND LIST. Gillian and her friends make a list of the *ton's* most likely bachelors, but they're all unacceptable to her—until she meets the very sexy . . . and wildly unattainable . . . Earl of Shelbrooke.

It's evening, you've just settled down, there's a knock at the door—you open it, and could it be Mr. Right? In Hailey North's PERFECT MATCH pretty Lauren Stevens not only has one man vying for her affections . . . she has two—and to make matters more complicated, they're brothers! But for Lauren, Alistair Gotho is nothing but trouble . . .

Go west, young woman! And Rachelle Morgan's MUSTANG ANNIE is the perfect western gal—sexy, sassy . . . and determined not to fall for any old cowpoke that comes her way. But handsome Brett Corrigan is anything but old . . . he's completely irresistible.

Maximilian Chartwell made a promise he'd always protect his young cousin the duke, and he's not about to let an upstart American heiress trap the impressionable lad into marriage. But in Marlene Suson's NEVER A LADY it's Max himself who just might get trapped.

Enjoy!

Lucia Macro

Lucia Macro
Executive Editor
Avon Romance

Avon Romantic Treasures

*Unforgettable, enthralling love stories,
sparkling with passion and adventure
from Romance's bestselling authors*

MY BELOVED
by Karen Ranney
80590-1/$5.99 US/$7.99 Can

THE BRIDE OF JOHNNY MCALLISTER
by Lori Copeland
80248-1/$5.99 US/$7.99 Can

HAPPILY EVER AFTER
by Tanya Anne Crosby
78574-9/$5.99 US/$7.99 Can

THE WEDDING BARGAIN
by Victoria Alexander
80629-0/$5.99 US/$7.99 Can

THE DUKE AND I
by Julia Quinn
80082-9/$5.99 US/$7.99 Can

MY TRUE LOVE
by Karen Ranney
80591-X/$5.99 US/$7.99 Can

THE DANGEROUS LORD
by Sabrina Jeffries
80927-3/$5.99 US/$7.99 Can

THE MAIDEN BRIDE
by Linda Needham
79636-8/$5.99 US/$7.99 Can

A TASTE OF SIN
by Connie Mason
80801-3/$5.99 US/$7.99 Can

THE MOST WANTED BACHELOR
by Susan K. Law
80497-2/$5.99 US/$7.99 Can

....

Available wherever books are sold or please call 1-800-331-3761
to order.   RT 0300